# Toygasm

It's a case of mistaken identity when Josh and Jode, co-owners of a lucrative toy business, show up for a photo shoot with famous model Cammie Creek.

Cammie believes the two hunks are the men she's supposed to pose with.

Usually she doesn't mix business with pleasure, but when they're being naughty with her right in front of the cameras, she can't resist turning them into her personal toys.

Josh and Jode can't get enough of Cammie—how will she react when she discovers they're actually her bosses?

Toygasm
Published by Spunky Girl Publishing
Copyright 2016 by Jan Springer
Discover other titles by Jan Springer at http:www.janspringer.com
Edited by Julie Naughton

Licence Note
This ebook is permitted for your personal use only.
Author Note
This is a work of fiction. Characters, places, settings and events
presented in this book are purely of the author's imagination and bear
no resemblance to any actual person, living or dead or to any actual
events, places and/or settings.

Please note: Toygasm has been previously published under the same title.
First Edition 2013
Second Edition 2016

# Chapter One

*Devin Creek, Massachusetts*

JODE AND JOSH, NEW owners of adult toy manufacturer Sexy Toys, stared at the tastefully done photos plastered along the walls of their company's main conference room. In each of the framed black-and-white shots, an alluring seminude dark-haired woman held provocative poses with some of the company's original adult toy products. Just looking at her made Jode's cock swell and push violently against the tight restraints of his pants. Thanks to the emotional connection they'd shared since birth, he could feel his brother's similar reaction.

Like a storm, it washed over them. An intensity to dominate her. A craving to double-penetrate her. To claim her as their own.

It was times like these he wished they didn't share this intense physical bond. It was rare that they responded so strongly to the same woman. As a matter of fact, this woman was the first they'd reacted this sensually to and they were almost coming in their pants.

*Whoa. This girl is hot*, Josh whispered into Jode's mind.

*She's a scorcher*, Jode replied. *Just looking into her eyes I'll buy anything from her.*

"Who is this woman in all these photos?" Jode blurted to the office staff who waited noisily in the conference room for him and his partner to lay out the campaign for putting Sexy Toys back on top of the erotic toy industry.

At his question, the entire room, all twenty of the company's office staff, fell silent.

"That's Cammie Creek. She was the company's first model. She was one of the founders too," replied his forty-five-year-old assistant, Kim Jones.

*Sexy as sin.* His brother chuckled.

"That would make her how old? Forty?" Jode mentally calculated the age based on Cammie being twenty at the time these photographs were taken.

Kim nodded. His mind began to churn with possibilities. Cammie Creek would be perfect for their new launch. Timeworn meets new in their red-hot waterproof solar toy line.

"I want her." And he meant that quite literally. He wanted to meet her. To kiss her. Take her pussy into his mouth and suck on her clit until her cries of arousal filled the air. Man, he wanted her so bad, he was afraid his cock would never be the same. He ached like a son of a bitch. Cripes, he was even perspiring, and he never sweated under pressure. And, by golly, he was under sexual stress.

*Chill, bro. They're looking at you like you have two heads.* Josh chuckled into Jode's mind.

"Sir?" Kim whispered. Jode didn't miss the sudden uneasy look Kim threw Earl, Sexy Toys' elderly sales manager.

Earl smiled back at her like the cat who'd eaten the canary.

Instinctively, Jode got the feeling there was some nasty history between Earl and Cammie. Just the thought of this man being anywhere near her made his protective instincts awaken like never before.

"For the Red Line launch. I want her as the female model." He needed to find out more about her.

*We need to find out more about her*, his brother corrected.

"She's way too old for our products," Earl said quickly.

He pushed his chair from the conference table, stood and sidled in between Josh and Jode.

Both Jode and Josh tensed as Earl surveyed the photos. There was something not right in the leering way this man stared at Cammie Creek. The elderly man's short tongue licked at his chubby lower lip. His pale-blue eyes glared with too much appreciation at a photo of Cammie kissing the tip of a giant black flesh-like dildo. His satisfied smirk irritated Jode and he sensed rage bubbling in his brother as well.

*Why do I want to punch his face in?* Josh snapped.

*Easy, bro. Take a number.*

Huh, interesting reactions they were having.

"She was quite famous," Earl continued. The smug tone in his voice seemed inappropriate. To tell the truth Jode didn't even want this man talking about her.

"I'm surprised you've never heard of her," Earl continued. "But then again, the Midnight brothers were barely out of diapers when she was here lovingly stroking all those toys."

"We didn't buy this business based on our knowledge of the history of Sexy Toys, but on our experience in turning a declining firm around. Now who is she and why isn't she available?" Josh asked in a commanding voice that impressed Jode.

That's what the Midnight brothers did. They were thirty years old and for the last six years they'd made millions purchasing faltering companies and turning them around until they made hefty sales again—and then they sold them at massive profits. This place was their latest project.

"I said she's too old," Earl ground out between gritted teeth.

"I said I want her for the campaign," Jode said with a sternness that had Earl's eyes widening with surprise.

"She's probably not even modeling anymore." Irritation laced Earl's voice.

"Are you saying you can't get her?"

"She quit us a long time ago."

*Interesting. With looks like hers, Earl probably made a play for her,* Josh commented internally.

"What's the matter? Did she turn you down?" Jode asked, grabbing on to Josh's idea.

Anger flashed across Earl's face.

*Bingo.*

"She's past her prime," Earl stated coldly.

"I could say the same about you, Earl," Josh replied with a frostiness that had the entire staff sitting quiet as mice, their attention focused on the confrontation.

Red flushed the man's wrinkled cheeks.

"We need a young, vibrant model for the Red Line is what I am saying and Cammie is washed-up," Earl said in a barely controlled voice.

Jode was about to tell Earl that he was a dirty old man who wanted a young, vibrant model so he could jump her innocent bones. However, before he could retaliate, a light touch to his elbow from his brother reined him in. The frowns on most of the older staff members' faces showed they were not amused. He needed to smooth things over and fast. This early in the game, he didn't want to lose their respect.

"Sexy Toys is over the hill too," he stated gently. "Our products are old, but they are good. That's why our sales are still okay, but they are, as you've been informed by the previous owner, declining. This place needs a shot in the arm. We need better sales to keep this company open and to keep you all working. With our idea of making the old toys going solar-charged, we need a familiar face to draw attention to us. In this case being old is to our advantage. We'll get Cammie Creek to model for us."

"Good luck." Earl guffawed.

"Translation?" Josh asked coolly.

*Never show the employees you're pissed. Our number-one rule,* his brother warned.

*Fuck off. The guy is an asshole.*

*Easy. They're watching.*

Josh nodded. But Jode could feel his brother's anger despite what he was saying.

"I'm telling you she won't give you the time of day, Mr. Midnight."

*What's his problem?*

*Let me take care of this, Josh.*

*Be my guest.*

"Are you saying she'll be a challenge?" Jode never turned down a challenge.

Earl gave a short laugh. "Hell, I'm so sure Cammie Creek will tell you where to go with your idea I'm willing to bet my job she'll turn you down flat."

*Now there's a spectacular proposal.* Josh chuckled.

Jode could hear a pin drop. The people in the room were too silent. There was definitely some history between Sexy Toys and Cammie.

"What you're saying is if she accepts the job you'll turn in your resignation?"

Earl nodded stiffly, appearing to suddenly be not so sure of himself. "But I get to keep my company pension," he said.

This was too good an opportunity to turn down. Despite the two of them being new here, Earl had been a pain in their ass with his unbelievably smug know-it-all loud attitude. On a couple of occasions, they'd talked about firing him but he had a damned good sales record and he really hadn't done anything wrong except be arrogant.

*And an asshole*, Josh reminded him.

"Your offer is too tempting, Earl. I'll take you up on it," Jode stated.

Surprise splashed over Earl's face and Josh chuckled.

*He's an idiot*, Josh commented.

*Yeah, but the bastard has been with the company since the beginning. He has a shitload of contacts. He knows his stuff and we may need him to keep this company from going under. I shouldn't have accepted the bet. I was irresponsible.*

*It's your call.*

*Thanks for your help*, Jode replied snarkily.

*You're welcome.*

Jode squashed the urge to glare at his brother. Instead, he looked at another picture of Cammie.

There was something vulnerable in her looks and in the sweet way she seduced the camera. There was an innocence about her that cranked up Jode's protectiveness, despite the photo of her being twenty years old. She would have changed in the meantime, especially if she'd given up the strict regime required to be a model. But he was going to take a chance on her. He was so crazy about her or maybe he was just crazy, falling for a photo of a woman.

*Join the club*, Josh said softly.

"Okay, start packing your stuff, Earl. I'll have the photos of Cammie Creek posing with Sexy Toys' new Red Line by the end of this week."

Earl's frown turned upside down a little too quickly for Jode's comfort. Maybe the prick had set him up?

"Not so fast, Mr. Midnight."

*Uh-huh. Should have known this was too good to be true*, Josh commented.

*Let's hear what he has to say.*

*Let's not.*

*Just relax.*

Before his brother could retort, Earl spoke.

"If I'm putting my job on the line, then I'll expect the same from you two."

"That's fair."

*Like hell. I'm not supposed to be in on this. This smells fishy*, his brother complained.

*We're in this together. Let's hear what he has to say.*

Earl chuckled with that familiar smugness that irritated Jode.

"Perhaps the both of you should start packing, Mr. Midnight. I'm betting Cammie will say no to a photo shoot and if she does, you give me the company. No strings. Free."

*Fuck!* His brother's curse echoed painfully in his mind.

Jode caught his brother's gaze. His face went red with rage.

*Quiet. I'll handle this,* he chided Josh.

*Shit! What if Earl knows something about Cammie that we don't? What if she's some hausfrau with a shitload of kids and she is totally out of modeling?*

Jode gazed back at a photo of Cammie with a string of pearl-shaped anal beads lying across her perky breasts.

"Was she a runner?" he asked as he cast a glance at his assistant, Kim. She didn't look too worried. She'd been here as long as Earl and she must know something about Cammie.

"Yes, she was, but we've lost touch over the years," Kim answered.

*Where are you going with this?* his brother asked.

*Serious runners tend to stick to it, especially once they encounter runner's high. Running is hard to give up after that. Besides, it keeps one in shape. Am I right?*

Both Josh and Jode ran seven miles every morning before indulging in a high-protein breakfast at a local health food restaurant.

*Yeah, but anything could have happened to her in the meantime. She may not even be seriously into it like us,* Josh warned.

*She's a runner, that's all I need to know. And with our combined reaction to her, trust me— we're going to be a perfect fit.*

Damned if his assistant didn't suddenly give him a slight nod to go ahead. At least he hoped that's what she meant as she smiled along with that nod.

*Unless it's her way of placating you and letting you know you're fucking insane,* Josh chided.

*Then we'll have to move fast on this before someone tips Cammie off to the bet.*

He didn't want to lose.

*But we do want to lose Earl*, his brother reminded him.

"Okay, we have a deal," Josh suddenly said. To Jode's surprise, his brother shook the older man's hand.

*What the fuck? Shaking hands with the enemy, bro?* he said to Josh.

*You know what they say. Keep your friends close, but keep your enemies closer.*

Earl laughed and then he shouted to the staff members, "You are all my witnesses. Remember what you heard here."

Some of the employees whooped for Earl whereas others frowned, appearing as if they didn't think the bet was such a good idea.

His brother slapped Earl on the back.

"Good luck, my man," he said to the elderly man.

Earl looked stunned and for a moment his smile dropped into a frown, but he quickly smiled again and sat back down in his chair.

"Wish I could say the same." He laughed and looked at the rest of the group, an arrogant smirk on his pudgy face.

*No one fucks with a Midnight man*, Josh commented to Jode as he went to sit on his chair at the head of the table so they could get their meeting started.

*Not unless a Midnight man wants to be fucked*, Jode replied, feeling excitement tear through him at the bet and at soon meeting Cammie Creek.

He definitely didn't want to be fucked by Earl. Cammie Creek, on the other hand...

· · ୶ · ·

"WHAT DO YOU MEAN YOU don't think she'll go for it?" Jode snapped as Josh walked quietly down the deserted hallway toward Jode's office. It was long after quitting time and everyone had gone home. The only ones left in the building were Josh, Jode and their assistant Kim.

Desperation whipped off Jode and seared into Josh as he neared his brother's office. Quietly Josh peeked into the open office doorway and discovered Kim sitting in the chair opposite Jode's office desk. Her shoulders were stiff with tension and her hands were knotted in her lap. From the frown marring her perfectly shaped lips, this was the last place she wanted to be. And from the severe scowl etching Jode's face, he didn't like what Kim was telling him.

"Like Earl said, Cammie doesn't model anymore. At least, I don't think she does. We lost touch when she left here," she replied.

"Then why in hell were you nodding in the conference room?"

*I misread her signals,* Jode's voice echoed in his mind as he caught sight of Josh.

*Don't jump to conclusions. Let's just see what she has to say.*

Jode sighed heavily.

Kim shrugged.

"I was caught up in the moment. I was thrilled you were sticking up for Cammie and I was just trying to reassure you that you were doing the right thing."

"And the right thing is?" Jode prodded.

Her voice lowered. "Cammie won't come back as long as Earl is here. They have...a history. And I am sorry, but I won't betray Cammie's confidence by saying anything else."

*Like hell she won't. She'll tell us everything.* Jode's thought snapped in Josh's mind.

Josh tried hard to push away Jode's anger, but it wasn't working. It slithered through him like an angry serpent. Their instincts about Earl doing Cammie some harm had been spot-on.

"The only way we can get rid of Earl is to get Cammie into our camp," Josh said as he stepped into the room and closed the door behind him.

Jode didn't bother to look up. Hell, he always sensed when Josh was around, so it would be no surprise to him that Josh had been listening at the door. Kim, on the other hand, just about jumped out of her chair.

"Why so nervous, Kim?" Josh asked as he came to stand beside her.

"You startled me, that's all." She kept her gaze down at her clenched hands.

Jode frowned.

*Something's spooked her.*

*You mean someone.*

*Earl,* they whispered in unison.

"What's Earl got on you?" Josh asked. Might as well get straight to the point.

Kim's face crumpled and, to Josh's shock, tears glistened in her brown eyes.

*What the fuck? You made her cry?* Jode teased.

"I can't say. I don't want to lose my job. My husband died years ago. I have no family besides my two kids. They love it here. All our friends are here. This job is the best-paying one available in this small town. I don't know where else we can move. If Earl wins this bet, I'm gone. He's..." Her lower lip trembled so badly that Josh instantly grabbed a tissue from Jode's desk and handed it to her. She dabbed at the sides of her eyes.

"He's one of those men..." she sobbed.

Josh stared at Jode looking for an answer. His brother shrugged.

*Don't look at me. I don't know what she means, except for what I can come up with in my imagination. And those scenarios are all bad,* Jode said.

"It's why Cammie left...or rather why she was forced to leave." She blew her nose into the tissue.

*Forced to leave. I want to kill Earl,* Jode growled.

*Back down. She's on the verge of hysteria. We can question her tomorrow when she's feeling better.*

*Tomorrow is Saturday. We can't ask her to leave her kids on the weekend.*

*You're right. Leave it until Monday.*

"I've already said too much. I can't say more. I don't want a defamation of character lawsuit on my hands. I should go..." She stood and walked past Josh. She opened the door and then hesitated.

"You can contact Cammie's agent, Alison Kent. Her number is in my database. You already have my password. You can tell her that I sent you. I don't know if she'll reveal Cammie's whereabouts. She left town abruptly years ago and didn't leave anyone a forwarding address."

*No forwarding address? Must have been something really serious,* Jode murmured.

"Alison will be able to tell you if Cammie is still available. If I were you two, I would hurry before Earl finds her first. The bet you made with him will make him even more aggressive than he already is."

Josh nodded. The now-familiar twist of desperation raged through him yet again. It seemed as if Earl was a bigger monster than they'd originally thought.

"You heard the lady. We'd better move fast," Jode said after Kim left the room.

"I'm already on it," Josh replied and quickly headed to Jode's computer.

•• ❧ ••

"THINK ARTISTIC NUDE with toy insertions. Think sex. Red-hot sex with two scrumptious males and Sexy Toys' Past meets Future Red line of solar-powered toys," Cammie Creek's red-haired agent Alison Kent said excitedly. Alison had called late last night insisting they get together for a breakfast meeting because she was taking the Acela from New York and she had a job opportunity Cammie would not be able to pass up.

Now they sat at Cammie's favorite downtown Philadelphia breakfast bar, sipping green tea and munching blueberry bagels doused with the bar's ultra-delicious blueberry cream cheese as a wicked nervousness raced through her. Sexy Toys wanted her back after all these years.

"They're thinking videos, toy trailers, advertisement layouts in all the major toy magazines and websites. The works. As I said, the new owners want only you. And they want you yesterday." Alison nodded to the arrangement of papers Cammie was sifting through.

"I met with the owners last night. They are really eager to meet you. They said they saw your photos in the conference room. Those two men are so hot, sexy and young. I know a secret about them, but you'll know what it is when you see them."

*A secret*? Before Cammie could question her, Alison continued.

"I like their vision. Past embraces future. You're from their past. A successful past, I might add, and their new line sounds impressive. You'll work exclusively with the two owners and the male models. I told them you have a gorgeous house filled with gorgeous rooms so they can use it for their shoot and they agreed. As you've seen there's a property release form in there too along with the model release agreement."

"Alison..."

"I know, I know. You guys had a falling-out years ago, but this money is just way too good to give up. Earl is not involved in the shoot. The new owners have promised not to let him know your whereabouts."

"Do they know what happened?" Surely they didn't or they wouldn't be asking for her services. There was no way Earl would allow it.

"Honey, everything was kept hush-hush back then."

"Except for Earl, who continued bad-mouthing me to everyone who'd listen. I should have gone to the cops."

"He's just an asshole."

Sudden rage tore through her. "That asshole almost ruined my modeling career with him stalking me and he screwed me out of my rightful part-ownership of Sexy Toys!"

Alison shifted uneasily in her seat as she looked around the bar. Cammie realized she'd snapped too loudly and some of the patrons were observing them.

Cammie lowered her voice. "Sorry, but I got the shitty end of the stick. I didn't have the confidence to do the right thing back then. He's still working there and I've been chasing peanuts and keeping a low profile. I loved that job. I helped start that business and then I was out on my ass when the shit hit the fan."

Alison's eyes twinkled with mischief.

"Of course I will get them to double the offer before accepting..."

Double the offer? Cammie's head spun. She wasn't worth that much. Was she? Defiance blossomed inside her. Heck yes, she was worth that much. She'd been good at her job as an erotic model for Sexy Toys. She'd made herself the figurehead of that business, making sure she was front and center with Sexy Toys' toys at all the conventions. Sales had skyrocketed when she'd been with the company.

"They owe you big-time for allowing you to leave. If you accept the double offer, then you can get that custom-made two-car garage with that huge studio loft you've been dreaming about."

Alison paused for effect and Cammie knew it was to let it sink in about the garage and loft. For that past few years her modeling jobs were becoming fewer and fewer. In this business younger models were more popular. She realized that. Understood the industry.

She'd done all the right things in keeping herself fit. She'd taken good care of herself by eating balanced meals, continuing her running regime and doing yoga and mind relaxation exercises. She'd banked money for her retirement, paid off her home and at forty-two she was ready to start a new career. She just didn't know what.

Yet here was Alison making her a lucrative offer she could only have dreamed of until this proposal.

Alison continued, her smile dipping into a grimace. Cammie tensed. *Oh great, something* is *wrong. It sounded too good to be true.*

"There's one little hitch. They want everything done by the end of this coming week. So by Friday morning."

End of this week! It was Sunday. The woman was crazy! She couldn't do this in such a short time. Photo shoots took hours to do and that was with just one toy. It appeared from this proposal that the company had at least twenty new toys. It would take days and most likely a couple of nights too to meet that deadline. Besides, she needed a waxing and to have her hair done.

Cammie forced herself to inhale several deep breaths to calm down. She set aside the proposal and studied the contract once more. They were offering such an incredibly large amount of money. And now Alison wanted to double it. Sexy Toys wanted her back, even after their history. She'd left them on bad terms but if there was new management...and no Earl involved...

"Unless you don't think you can handle this..." Alison challenged softly. Her smile had returned. This time with a taunting edge.

The last thing Cammie would ever admit to Sexy Toys—or her agent, for that matter—was that she couldn't meet a deadline. She was a professional and she always met her deadlines. But even after all these years she was still as insecure as hell in the erotic photography world mainly because of what had happened with Earl.

Truth was she welcomed the insecurity. It kept her focused, not to mention her ego intact. And having a recent Sexy Toys shoot in her portfolio would dispel any rumors that might still be circulating about that bad split between them. She knew she'd lost way too many jobs because of it and because of Earl.

"No problem," she lied. "But make it triple and I want creative input. If they agree to those conditions, then I will accept their offer."

Alison didn't even flinch at her demand.

"Excellent! I knew I could count on you. Consider it a done deal on the triple amount and artistic input. I'll have them make the amendments. Oh! And I gave the company your address."

"What? How did you know I was going to say yes?"

Alison winked.

Without waiting for a response her agent stood and signaled to their waitress for the check. Then she refocused her attention to Cammie. Her gray eyes flashed with confidence.

"Work your magic, Cammie. You'll do great. I've got to run now, I have to catch the Acela back to New York for another meeting. Ta-ta, darling."

Cammie watched Alison meet up with the waitress, pluck the check out of her hand and then head to the cashier. After paying the bill, she threw Cammie a final wave and then she was gone.

Reality crashed in on Cammie. Sure, she was in okay shape for toy inserts, but the rest of her wasn't as slim as she'd once been. How in the world was she going to pull this off?

# Chapter Two

*Hearttowne, Pennsylvania*

SHE'D CERTAINLY PUT a good dent into cleaning and straightening up her home as well as sprucing up her looks, Cammie mused as she stared into the full-length mirror hung on her upstairs bathroom door. She wore a smart, curve-hugging chocolate-brown dress with white scallop trim. She'd pinned her hair into a sexy updo with several soft ringlets dangling down both sides of her face and she'd dabbed a touch of her favorite perfume on her wrists and her neck.

It was a stroke of luck Alison had mentioned Cammie's home to Sexy Toys. It meant no travel time to other destinations for her and they could work as late as needed. Her home, a quaint two-story cottage, was set on a secluded rocky peninsula and overlooked a small, private Pennsylvania lake. The house consisted of a fully modernized kitchen, a charming living room with nook, two full bathrooms, one on the main floor and the other upstairs, and four large bedrooms—three upstairs and one on the main floor beside the kitchen. On clear September days such as today, bright sunshine streamed in all the windows.

She was glad she'd told Alison she wanted creative input because when she eyed the dreamy daybed in the sun-washed nook against the large bay window, overlooking a quiet backdrop of lush pine trees and allowing generous peeks of the blue lake. Cammie knew this area would be a perfect spot for one of the shoots.

After leaving the breakfast bar in town this morning, she'd headed directly to the bank machine and deposited her advance check. Then to her favorite salon, where she'd been lucky enough to get an immediate waxing on her intimate parts. After that, she'd gone home and was surprised to discover several large boxes piled in her home's side entrance. The items and letter were from the new owners. They had said they would be dropping by late afternoon. Today!

She'd taken the initiative to order food to be delivered to the house later tonight for the photo crew. She had the feeling they would be working through dinner and late into tonight in their need to put a dent into meeting that deadline. She was putting the finishing touches on her blush when a snappy knock at the front door rocked Cammie back to her senses.

*Shit!* They were here! With one final look into the mirror, she nodded at a job well done and forced herself to smile. Yes, outwardly she looked pretty good. Inwardly, her tummy twisted with nervous tension.

Had she been crazy to accept this gig? She shook her head. No, this was her job. She was used to having strange men ogling her private parts. She would remain professional and polite. She could do this gig with Sexy Toys. Couldn't she?

The sharp rap came again, this time louder and more insistent.

"Coming!" she called out.

She forced herself not to run down the stairs but kept herself reined into a brisk walk, mostly because the last thing she wanted to do was to fall and break something. Sweet heavens, now *that* would be embarrassing.

A moment later, with a shaky hand, she gripped the doorknob, inhaled a deep breath to steady her rattling nerves and whipped open the door. The air rushed out of her lungs in one intoxicating whoosh. Quite the handsome men stood in front of her. Identical twins who appeared to be in their late twenties or early thirties.

Something wild and hot sizzled in the air between her and them. Instant attraction? No way. Not possible. Yet her tummy fluttered with awesome butterflies and her breath came in incredibly short bursts.

Their eyes were as blue as the September sky above. White, even teeth flashed as they both smiled. They were incredibly tall and chest muscles bunched beneath their casual white shirts.

*Wow. Hot hunks.*

The closest man held out his hand.

"Hi, we're—"

"No, don't tell me. Let me guess. You're the male models for the shoot," Cammie blurted as his warm palm melted against hers and they shook hands.

Nice grip. Large hand. A good-sized palm to hold her breasts or stroke her pussy, not to mention work a toy into her ass or cunt for the shoot.

Whew, her thoughts were going haywire! Heat flushed through her like a tidal wave.

"Actually we're—" he began, but she cut him off again as she let go of his hand and reached out to shake hands with the other model.

"Twins. What an awesome idea for the photo shoot," she complimented them.

Mercy, she was way too tense. She tended to cut people off in conversations when she was nervous, just as she was doing now.

She stared at one man and then the other. Identical. She could not tell them apart if her life depended on it. They wore their hair the same. Semi-long dark-brown hair brushed straight back off their foreheads. They possessed plump, kissable lips. Flawless noses that weren't too long or too short. Their perfectly arched eyebrows were dark, and they had sexy shadows lining their chins and cheeks.

Eye-candy men she could drool over all day and all night. Sexy Toys had picked the perfect male models. And she would be working with them. Thankfully, they were just the models, so she didn't need to be totally professional. She could flirt a little and loosen up around them. She always liked to get to know the guys she'd be working with. It was so much easier that way when the time came for the intimate shoots.

"No one else has shown yet," she said. "But I'm sure they'll be along shortly. How about some coffee while we wait? Just have a seat in the living room and I'll be right with you."

She needed an excuse to get away for a moment and collect herself. She hadn't expected the models to be so good-looking. Or for her to feel so sexually attracted to them. Both of them!

She ushered them toward the living room and then quickly headed for the kitchen. After plugging in the coffeemaker, she grabbed an ice-cold bottle of water from the fridge and downed it in a few quick swallows.

*Okay, calm down*, a stern voice whispered at the back of her brain. *You've got to be professional.*

Coffee. Yes, she needed to get some coffee into her. Where coffee gave other folks the jitters, it had the opposite effect on her. It calmed her. Right now she needed calm. Thank goodness for coffee.

. . ❧ . .

*SHE'S EVEN MORE BEAUTIFUL than in her pictures. Twenty years has made her breathtaking*, Jode said to Josh as they both sat down on a white leather couch.

*I'm hard as a spike for her after meeting her just now. I know she's the woman for me.*

*For us*, Jode corrected.

*She thinks we're the male models.*

*I guess we should set her straight and tell her everything*, Jode replied. Although that was the last thing he wanted to do. Guilt at not laying out the truth to her ran a naughty thread through him, but it might be better to let her believe they were the models.

*Well technically, Jode, we are the models and the photographer, thanks to the fact we haven't been able to find the company's regular photographers. And with the male model we'd decided to use conveniently taking an unexpected trip and our agencies not having anyone available at such short notice, it's a good thing I know all the ins and outs of this industry, including professional photography.*

*Quit your bragging, bro. I'll be the lucky one, as I'll be with her and the toys and not behind the camera like you.* Jode chuckled.

*Au contraire, timers on the cameras will allow me as much face time with her as you.*

*Well, okay, you have me there,* Jode admitted. *Two guys would be better than one for her. She would get twice the pleasure.*

*She does have a very nice place here. A quaint, cozy modern look with pale colors, and that sun-drenched nook over there is a bit bright but with the proper diffuser lens...*

*Enough shop talk, Josh. I don't want to hear it. And please don't go telling her everything about your photo skills or you'll bore her to death too,* Jode teased his brother.

Josh quirked an eyebrow at him and appeared properly insulted.

*I never bore a woman,* he replied.

"And we most definitely don't want Cammie uninterested in us. I think Earl did us a huge favor in conveniently making all the people we needed for the shoot unreachable," Jode said.

He'd switched to a low voice so Cammie couldn't hear. Talking with their minds used a lot of energy and they needed to save their vitality for her.

"He probably paid the model himself for that trip and sent the rest of the crew on a trip somewhere too at his expense, thinking he already owns Sexy Toys," Josh said.

"Yeah, he's probably sitting somewhere with his legs set leisurely up on a table, sipping back some cognac and toasting to his good luck at this bet. Let's make sure he doesn't win."

"Hell, if we end up getting the luscious lady in the end, then we've won. To hell with Sexy Toys," Josh replied matter-of-factly.

Why did he get the feeling that Josh had already fallen so deeply for Cammie that he couldn't even think straight?

"But sticking it to Earl would be the icing on a very delicious cake, don't you think?" he reminded his brother.

Josh's eyes lit up like one of those bright candles on said cake.

"I like the way you think, bro. Let's get this show on the road."

• • ∞ • •

THE SEX-ON-A-STICK twins stopped talking when Cammie walked into the room. She'd prepared a tray laden with coffee and slices of her favorite vanilla cake. In the kitchen, she'd been trying to listen in to what they'd been whispering about, but their voices were so low, she hadn't been able to make out heads or tails except for the mention of cake. That's why she'd decided to serve them some.

"You're glowing," one of the male models commented as they both stood.

She was glowing? Mercy, manners would get them everywhere with her. She placed the tray onto the coffee table in front of them and resisted the urge to place her hands on her hot cheeks.

"I...thank you." Was that an appropriate response? What did he mean by glowing? Was she so visibly nervous that she was blushing?

He nodded and then the other man swept his hand to the open spot on the couch between them.

"Please have a seat here."

Between them? Like the female filling to a man sandwich? A ménage. With an abundance of sex toys. To her annoyance, her cheeks grew hotter.

That's when she noticed the sensual upward curves of both men's full lips.

Oh boy, if looks could seduce they would be fucking her right now on her couch. She blinked that insane thought away. Why in the world did she even think they wanted to have sex with her? They'd just met her.

They were male models doing a job. But she sure was thinking about sexing them. It wasn't unheard of for her to hook up with a male model and have sex during a photo shoot. It was very rare but she had done it. The erotic tension of being naked with a hot sexy man and toys being inserted into her sometimes got the better of her. But she'd never done it with two men before!

*Down, girl.* She needed that coffee. Now.

Before she could ask them how they took their coffee, the man on her right side reached out to serve.

"By the way, I'm Josh and this here is Jode. How do you take yours?" He nodded to the coffee.

"Black. Thank you, Josh."

She sat down between them and tried hard to ignore the incredible heat whipping against her body from the duo. They smelled nice. Mild spice with a hint of soap.

Josh placed a cup in front of her on the table and she couldn't get to it fast enough.

"Any idea when the others will get here?" she asked after she took an abundance of sips of the hot liquid.

Ah, wonderful. Coffee hit the spot. Relaxation was already whispering over her.

"Actually, they won't be coming," Jode replied.

Her relaxation vanished and devastation rocked her. She had to be careful not to swallow too quickly, lest she choke.

"Not coming?" Had she heard right? She almost swore out loud in her disappointment as her garage and studio loft seemed to sift right out of her fingers. Frig! She'd already deposited the advance check Alison had given her this morning.

"Not to worry, though," Josh said quickly, picking up her alarm. "Something came up. The three of us will be responsible for getting everything done and in to the company on time. Do you think you're up for the challenge?"

This was highly unusual. She was used to a film crew. Familiar with people who played with lights. Coaches. Photographers. Makeup artists. Stylists. Wardrobe.

"I did ask for creative input," she blurted.

"We've been briefed on everything by Alison. We have the amendments Alison said you wanted and they are ready for you to sign. We'll love any and all of your input," Jode said from her other side.

Well, that was interesting.

Without warning, Josh leaned closer, and she held her breath as he brushed a stray strand of hair from her face. Instead of pulling away, he leisurely stroked her cheek. His tender touch sent shivers of need coursing through her. She noted his exceptionally long fingers. Clean. Well-trimmed fingernails. Perfect finger-fucking fingers. She raised her gaze to discover him studying her with the most intense blue eyes she'd ever seen. Eyes that said "let's undress and make love."

*Oh, Cammie! Stop! Focus on the assignment, woman!*

"Sexy Toys was right. You are the perfect model," Jode replied in a sultry voice. There was a tender pull on one of the strands at the back of her neck as if he was twirling a finger around her hair. "Your sparkling brown eyes and that cute Cupid's-bow mouth will melt any man's knees. Any woman will be envious when they see you having two men making love to you with the help of a box full of Sexy Toys products."

"We're not trying to melt a man's knees, we're trying to sell him sex toys. Orgasm with Sexy Toys, I believe Alison put it," she said breathlessly. She was warming way too much to their words and to their intoxicating nearness. Her breasts pressed snugly against her blouse and her nipples ached to be touched.

"I want you to have this sultry look for our first session. Dreamy, sexy and vulnerable," Josh whispered.

Dreamy, sexy and vulnerable? She blinked in surprise. Was she reading too much into this? Maybe they weren't flirting but coaching her for the shoot? Disappointment needled into her.

"We've seen your photos from the time you first started with them, and you are even more beautiful now," Jode said from the other side of her.

*Oh my, more compliments.*

"You're so sweet to say that," she gushed.

"It's true."

His eyes were sparkling a darker shade and she swore she could see her reflection in them. He continued twirling a strand of her hair. The sensual tug of pain on her scalp had her struggling to stop a moan from escaping.

*Oh dear. This feels very good.*

Josh stopped stroking her cheek and a serious, determined look crossed his face. Abandoning his untouched coffee, he stood and eyed the cozy nook she'd been pondering about suggesting to use in one of the shoots.

"Black velvet sheets and you masturbating while two men watch. It would look quite attractive in an ad," Josh said smoothly.

Cammie had no clue what to say. She was tongue-tied for the first time in her life. She *would* have them watching her masturbating. Any other time, it would be an automatic part of her job but this time it was different. The air crackled with a stimulating sexual tension. Way too much to be normal.

Josh smiled and a deep dimple popped out on his right cheek. Her breath caught and her tummy did a wonderful dip as if she were on a roller coaster. Oh my, she'd have to figure out how to keep him smiling. That cute dimple was to-die-for gorgeous.

When he caught her staring at him, he cleared his throat with a sweet nervousness.

"Jode, come on and give me a hand in getting the equipment out of the van. We need to get that light while we have it."

"I think the dual vibrator will be perfect for her first time," Jode said as he stood.

Her first time? Did they know she'd never been with two men before?

"Cammie, would you mind finding the dual vibrator and getting it ready for use? All the toys come pre-sterilized, but if you'd like to clean it just to make yourself comfortable, I believe it's labeled as being in box number one. All the toys are already charged, too, before they go into the packaging phase. 'Ready-to-go-toys' is one of our new mottos. Here's the list of all the items and which boxes they're in," Jode said as he pulled a sheet of paper from a back pocket and handed it to her.

"Sure thing." She tried hard not to sound tense or excited at working with these two guys but her voice came off as strained.

He nodded and his grin made a dimple pop out on his left cheek.

*Oh wow, that is so cute. Josh has a dimple in his right cheek and Jode has one in his left. That's how I can tell them apart!*

Her heart pounded a mile a minute as the front door closed behind them.

*Pull yourself together, woman. If you don't, then you'll end up taking these two hunks into your bed instead of earning the large amount of money Sexy Toys has offered for this contract.*

Maybe she was reading too much into how these two models seemed to be undressing her with their hot gazes? But...what if she wasn't?

• • ❧ • •

"DREAMY, SEXY AND...vulnerable?" Jode chuckled as he caught up with Josh at the van. Josh could tell by the laughter underlying Jode's voice that he was in a kidding mode, but Josh wasn't. He'd had to get away from Cammie or he'd have lost control and spilled his guts.

He would have explained who they were and the reason there was such a tight deadline. Besides, his cock was harder than a post and just being near Cammie had him wanting to know so much more about her. More than her just being in hot, intimate portraits on a wall in a conference room and him wanting to fuck her. She was even sexier in real life. Sexier than he could ever have imagined. She was also vulnerable and a dream to look at. He whipped open the back door of the van and began hauling out equipment.

"Well, it's true. She is all that," Josh replied as he handed Jode a large tripod and a couple of camera bags.

"Hell, I'm not complaining. It's just you are understating her beauty," Jode replied.

"Beauty, my man, is only skin deep," Josh growled.

"Ouch, now it's my turn to be insulted. I'm not that shallow."

Josh ignored him and hauled out a couple more bags and slammed the door shut. The way his balls hung so heavy beneath his cock had him struggling to walk straight as he started back toward the house.

"She's just too damned good to be true. She's the type of woman I could have only dreamed about until now," Josh confessed as Jode followed close behind him.

"And thousands of other men will be thinking the same thing when they see her spread out with those toys. Can you handle that?"

*No. I want her all for ourselves. This woman is ours.*

By the surprised look on Jode's face, Josh could tell his brother was thinking Josh was being way too intense. Jode's next words confirmed his suspicions.

*You need to keep things in perspective, Josh. She's not ours. Not yet, anyway. If we come on too strong to her, we'll scare her away. She seemed skittish sitting between us. And remember, we're complete strangers to her. Of course she's jumpy. She's also very attracted to us. She's fighting it, but not for long. Not if I can help it.*

*Not if I can help it either.* Josh picked up the pace so he could reach the door before Jode.

·· ❧ ··

FOR ALL THEY KNEW, Cammie was engaged or had a serious suitor. Jode had been telling himself these things over and over again so he wouldn't get his hopes up about Cammie. Until moments earlier, she'd just been a sexy woman in a picture to them. But basing their lust and any romantic feelings on merely a picture was wrong.

Saturday night during their meeting with Cammie's agent she'd been upfront about Cammie most likely refusing any offer if Earl was involved. She'd kept quiet about the history between Earl and Cammie, and upon learning that the man was not going to be involved in any way, Alison Kent had relaxed and given a bit of information about Cammie. But just as Kim had been, Alison was protective of Cammie, not saying too much about her personal life.

Alison told them that Cammie still ran. She kept herself in great shape due to her modeling career, she dated occasionally and she wasn't married. But that was as far as Alison had gone with Cammie's personal life, and they hadn't wanted to prod deeper or Alison would get suspicious, call the whole thing off and send them packing.

When they'd asked Alison if she knew of a great place for the shoot on such short notice, they'd been surprised that Alison had offered Cammie's historical home, assuring them it would meet with the expectations of the old-meets-new scenario.

Jode had been quite impressed by her home too. The outside of the two-story building was made from rustic granite rock. Bright-red shutters adorned all the windows and there was a white-painted wraparound porch with an abundance of hanging and potted flowers, from brilliant red geraniums to pristine white daisies. From the view in the driveway, he caught glimpses of a sparkling blue lake behind a shroud of white pine trees.

Best of all, no neighbors were in sight. This place was private and secluded and perfect for an adult toy photography shoot. He could hardly wait to get started.

• • ⚮ • •

CAMMIE'S NERVOUSNESS increased as she heard a quick rap on the door followed by the men entering her home.

"I'm in the bathroom. I'll be out in a minute," she called out.

Quickly she rinsed the soap off the toy that they would be using for the first segment. The dual vibrator was huge and so lifelike. The shafts were laden with elevated veins, and flesh-like material to the touch. If those men hadn't been in her house, she would have easily been able to pretend she was stroking two cocks.

Normally she wasn't shy around the photography crews, but with these two men, everything seemed too...intimate. Why was she reacting with such sexual interest to these guys? Maybe it had something to do with her not having had sex in quite some time?

She shook her head at that idea. She'd gone without for long bursts of time before. She wasn't in the habit of jumping into bed with just any guy, aside from the occasional model she had the hots for. She needed to have some feelings about him and some attraction. But with these two men her emotions were intertwined with fear, shyness, excitement, lust and everything in between.

After she dried the toy, she wrapped it in the towel. Hesitantly, she held it in her hands and left the main-floor bathroom. She was surprised to discover a couple of tripods with cameras already set up. Lights poised on stands were splashing onto the already-bright nook and the daybed had been transformed from her frilly white covers to the erotic tangle of shimmering black sheets that had been mentioned earlier. Obviously, the men had brought the sheets with them.

"Let's do some test shots first. I can check out the lighting and it will give you an opportunity to get more comfortable," one of the men said as he came out of her kitchen. A quick glance at the coffee table showed they'd removed the tray she'd brought out earlier.

"Jode's taking care of putting the cake in the refrigerator," he explained.

"That would make you Josh."

"The one and only. I'm also a professional photographer. It was one of my many extracurricular activities at university."

"What was your major?"

"Business. As with Jode. But unlike straitlaced me, he minored in partying and hangovers."

"Hey, that's not true." Jode erupted from the kitchen, a playful smile on his face. "Not fully true, anyway. I dabbled in partying, but not in hangovers. I know my limit."

"So how did you end up as models? Shouldn't you be working in something business-oriented?"

Both men tensed and for a moment they didn't say anything. Perhaps it was a touchy subject?

"Well, never mind. It's none of my business. Let's get rolling on the shoot, shall we?"

"I like a girl who's all business," Josh replied and winked at her as he stepped behind one of the cameras.

"Just hop on the bed, Cammie. Jode will coach you as to what needs to be done."

With her curiosity about the two men aroused, nervousness quickly pushed it aside and Cammie reached for the top button on her dress.

"No need to undress yet. Test shots only," Josh reminded her.

"Oh sorry. Right." Gosh, she was getting way too panicky. She had to calm down or they'd think she was some kind of shoddy amateur. She kicked off her high heels and to her surprise Jode touched her elbow and steered her toward the bed.

"The look we're going for in this nook is what Josh said earlier," Jode whispered.

"Dreamy, sexy and vulnerable," she replied.

As she remembered what had happened moments earlier while sitting between them on the couch, her breath moved into top speed and her mouth automatically parted as she panted softly.

"There you go—you already have that vulnerable expression we want," Jode said.

Excitement laced his soft, sultry voice as he continued. "Think ménage. Two hot, sexy men packed into one powerful dual vibrator."

Oh boy, he did have a way with words.

She sat down on the daybed and Jode instructed her into a sexy seated pose with her legs crossed. He unwrapped the toy from the towel and handed it to her. Then he walked back to stand beside Josh.

The two men studied her and exquisite heat flared.

"First I want you to stroke the vibe, sweetheart. Slowly, while I take test shots," Josh said. He ducked behind his tripod and camera.

Cammie nodded. Instinctively, she knew how to caress and how to hold a toy in an erotic pose against her body in front of a camera. She'd had years of experience, and it was second nature to her. The camera whirred as Josh snapped the shots.

"Beautiful. Perfect," Jode whispered.

He studied her and nodded approval with her every movement. She liked the sultriness of his low voice. It had an intimate feel, yet it put her at ease at the same time. Soon she slipped into the mood of lust and sex and making love with her hands to the vibrator. She caressed the weave of bulging veins and tenderly touched the mushroom-shaped cockheads.

Erotic moments like these were why she enjoyed her career and why she'd decided to specialize in erotic adult-toy modeling. She loved losing herself in the seductive whir of cameras and the sensual commands of coaches posturing her with incredibly sexy toys. For her, posing and having men and women admiring and complimenting her was similar to the high she experienced when she ran. Yet with modeling, she got paid to get high.

Her eyelids grew heavier. Her breath burst quicker past her slightly parted lips. She imagined Josh and Jode lying on the daybed with her, their naked thighs and muscular chests peeking out from the tangle of silky black sheets. Their big hands touching her body, stroking their fingers into her pussy and ass. Their mouths making love to her tight nipples. Both men then penetrating her at the same time.

"Okay, Cammie, the test shots look great. Now, let's get down to business," Josh's thick voice shattered through her, forcing her back to reality.

"How about you completely undress in the bathroom, put on a robe and come back out and we can take it from there?" Josh asked matter-of-factly.

She nodded and started as she caught Jode's intense stare. He was studying her with an I-want-to-devour-you expression. She lowered her gaze and caught sight of the bulge against the juncture of his pants.

Awesome size. Had that enormous erection been there earlier? Wouldn't she have noticed it before if it had? Was he that turned-on by the intimate way she'd handled the vibrator? She glanced at Josh, who was observing her with unmistakable lust in his eyes.

Oh dear. She had turned them on big-time.

She averted his gaze and hurried to the bathroom. Tension and wicked wariness whipped through her as she closed the bathroom door. Thankfully, she'd had the forethought to hang a robe in here, knowing there would be an initial awkward shyness until she got into the swing of the shoot.

Yes, that was what she had to be experiencing right now. The pre-shoot jitters. It's just she hadn't been so jumbled before.

She had a momentary lapse of wanting to call Alison to let her know what was going on. What would her agent say if she discovered

Sexy Toys had put the campaign into the hands of two male models and herself? What kind of business had they turned into that they allowed just anyone to run their show?

*But you aren't just anyone, Cammie,* an inner voice reminded her. *You used to be part of this corporation. You were a co-owner and it was at the top of its game with your input.*

Was that why Alison hadn't flinched when Cammie had asked for creative input? Because she had confidence in Cammie, confidence in her that had been shattered since her history with Earl? Dammit! She must not doubt her abilities. She could do this. She *would* do this. And if she encountered some wild hot sex along the way, so be it!

# Chapter Three

*SHE IS SO KILLING ME here*, Josh whispered. He resisted the overwhelming urge to reach into his pants, palm his engorged cock and bring himself some quick relief.

*And I'm not dying here also? The seductive way she strokes a vibe had me just about coming*, Jode complained. *How the hell are we going to handle it when she comes back and we go into the next phase? Her with no clothes?*

*Close-ups are going to be such a bitch*, Josh acknowledged.

Jode's sexual discomfort was seeping into Josh's body and wreaking havoc with his senses. How the hell were they going to handle Cammie?

He'd seen the faraway glaze of sensuality flow into her eyes as she'd gotten into the mood. Her pouty lips had parted in such a seductive way that he'd wanted to fuck her mouth right then and there. How in hell did professional photographers handle this type of job?

The click of the bathroom door opening echoed down the hallway.

*She's coming back out*, Jode warned. *A plan on how to handle this gorgeous woman should have been made before we came here. We should have known we'd react this way to her. Any suggestions on how to handle this?*

*None*, Josh admitted. The tension in his body inched up a few more degrees as his brother reacted to seeing Cammie enter the living room. She was clad in a fluffy white terrycloth robe. Even in a bathrobe she exuded sensuality.

*Oh crap. We are so screwed*, Jode whispered.

*Very screwed, indeed*, Josh agreed.

He cursed softly beneath his breath as Cammie began to untie the sash on her robe where she stood in front of the daybed.

"Something occurred to me while I was in the bathroom," Cammie said. A thrill of teasing excitement whipped through her. She was poised on the edge of an eagerness she'd never experienced before.

She wanted to flirt with these strangers. She hadn't wanted to do that in a long time. Suddenly she felt as if she were twenty again. Sexually free, playful and bouncing with sexual need.

"What's that?" Jode asked.

She detected nervous tension in his voice. Saw it in Josh too due to his watching her every movement as she sat on the daybed.

Perhaps they were picking up on her friskiness? From past experience she knew that allowing the crew to get a look at her intimate areas usually helped to break the tension. So she let the sides of the robe fall open. Both men's gazes snapped to the opening. She smiled and embraced the thrill of enthusiastic shivers as she observed their Adam's apples bobbing wildly as they swallowed.

In the past she'd learned to ignore the gawking and admiring looks as photographers and other members of a crew gazed upon her nudity. But for some curious reason with these two men, she had no idea how to disregard them or how to fully concentrate on the work at hand.

"I have a suggestion. If we're going to meet this deadline, we may need to double up on the toys. You two are twins, so why not go with the double theme? Instead of showcasing one item at a time, why not showcase two toys together? We can make it a theme of 'double your pleasure' or something like that. For instance, combine the dual vibrator with...say...labia clamps?"

"Labia clamps?" Jode murmured.

He gazed over at Josh, who shrugged his shoulders and nodded.

"We do have them. Red heart clamps that vibrate, actually," Josh replied in a tight voice. "And all charged and ready to go. Um, Jode, want to find them while I get Cammie positioned on the bed?"

"Coming right up." Jode began walking backward, appearing not be able to take his eyes off her.

The scorching way he stared at her was so endearing and intoxicating. It was empowering, too, that these two men, much younger than her, would be reacting so delightfully to her. When Jode crashed into the coffee table and stumbled, almost falling, she couldn't help but laugh at his clumsiness.

But her amusement stilled as Josh neared her. His intense blue eyes had her creaming.

"Let's get you into a similar position as you were moments ago. Keep the robe on but open it slightly, just as you have it now. We want to see the sexy curve of your inner thighs and a glimpse of your breasts. Men will be falling over their coffee tables when they get a look at this layout."

"Funny, ha ha," Jode grumbled as he untaped a box.

Josh winked at her and Cammie giggled.

She really liked the easygoing banter between these brothers and she appreciated Josh's attention to trying to make her feel more comfortable in their presence while in this attire. She wanted to reassure him that this modeling gig really was strictly professional. That she was a specialist and not the least bit embarrassed about being naked in front of them. But she couldn't bring herself to say it, because she'd be lying.

Truthfully, she was a bit shy around these two. It was the first time in a long time too. Whether that was a good thing or a bad thing, she wasn't sure. But she hoped it wouldn't interfere with her job.

"I'll clean these toys before we use them. I'll be back in a minute. And don't do anything without me." Jode disappeared down the hallway with a couple of packages in his hands.

"Wouldn't think of it," Josh breathed beside her. "I mean, the whole theme of the campaign is ménage, right?"

Sexual innuendo? Or a joke?

He didn't wait for her to answer.

"Okay, I need for you to move so you are sitting with your back pressed against the middle of the bay window. This will give potential customers a glimpse of the pine trees and the lake in the background."

His nearness unnerved her. His hot gaze gave her a fabulous craving to tease him too. She did as he asked and lifted her legs onto the bed. Raising her butt, she maneuvered around on the bed for several minutes until she was in a position he liked. Then she raised her knees just slightly so as to allow the men and the camera to see her breasts. Finally she opened her legs and tensed as Jode reentered the room.

"Perfect," Jode whispered as he approached her.

"She is, isn't she?" Josh said.

Both men stared at her and her cheeks warmed.

"Here are the clamps."

Jode held them up and Cammie smiled at the tiny clamps. Cute red hearts dangled from delicate gold chains. Jode was about to hand them to her when she shook her head.

"I think it would be better if you placed them on me."

"Shit," Josh whispered softly beneath his breath.

Jode's eyes widened and she swore if she blew a breath his way, he would topple right over.

Cammie could barely restrain a grin. These men were so cute! Aside from their reactions turning her on big-time, teasing them was fun.

"You should also plump the pussy lips. You know, so they'll look healthier in the pictures."

Both men totally tensed.

Huh, interesting. They seemed surprised at her request.

"Seriously. That's what is done. I'm sure you've seen this before in our line of work?"

She held her breath as Jode nodded slowly.

*Whew.* For a moment she'd been a wee bit worried these two men might actually be amateurs. But that couldn't be possible. The company would not give this campaign to two untested models.

"Okay," Jode said in a thick voice as he peered between her legs. But his lips suddenly quirked into a knowing grin.

Uh-oh. Was he on to her already? Was she that transparent in her teasing?

Cammie shuddered as Jode sat in front of her on the bed. His enticing spicy scent whispered around her and played havoc with her senses. What would it be like to have him kissing her? She held her breath as he laid the clamps onto the sheets.

Oh sweet mercy, this was incredibly sexy, watching him reach between her thighs.

She heard the whir of the camera. Realized that Josh was taking pictures of what was happening. Why? She didn't care. She just loved Jode's intense blue gaze and wanted his fingers on her pussy.

He touched her left labia, gripped it and then tenderly pulled her flesh. She couldn't stop the animalistic moan from escaping her mouth.

"You like?" Jode asked as he gazed up to study her face.

"It's...nice," she admitted.

He fell silent and plumped, tugged and massaged first one pussy lip and then the other. Shivers of pleasure whipped through her. He was good with his fingers and she fought hard not to gyrate her hips or arch her back.

She had not expected to be so aroused by his touch. But he was doing more than touching her pussy lips. It felt as if he were making love to them. Pulling and twisting, rubbing and kneading. Mercy, her breaths came faster and faster.

When he reached for the labia clamps, Cammie tensed.

"Hold still. I have a clit clamp to apply too," he whispered.

She closed her eyes and wished she could simply tell him to insert his finger into her vagina and thrust her into an orgasm. A moment later, there came the pinch of first one clamp and then the second as he efficiently placed them.

Then Jode began massaging her clit. Arousal burst through her and suddenly she wanted his face pressed between her legs.

*Oh my gosh. His touch is lethal.*

Cammie was so incredibly aroused, not to mention wet. Surely Jode would notice. Yet he remained tense and alert. With the flares of lust shining in his eyes as he worked her clit, he appeared quite interested in what he was doing. She creamed some more, unable to stop her reaction.

When she could stand it no more, when she was about to say to hell with everything and just start gyrating her hips, he suddenly stopped. She bit her bottom lip at the pinch of a clit clamp.

"Looks fantastic," Jode said in a hoarse whisper.

She opened her eyes to find his gaze heavy-lidded and brooding. Was he as frustrated as her? She breathed in deep, slow breaths, struggling to regain her composure.

"Ready?" he asked.

She nodded, cursing him for leaving her so needy. Had he done this on purpose? Or was she just reading things wrong?

"Okay, now I need to keep an eye on the lighting," Josh said. His voice sounded strangled and aroused. "I will do another round of test shots and then I'll go right into the shoot. Act natural and just keep going. Before you know it, Jode and I'll join you."

Oh sweet mercy. Join her? *I can't handle this. It's too incredibly arousing.*

Jode handed her the vibe she'd used earlier and once again there came a tremendous whirl of noises from the cameras.

Showtime. She became lost in seducing the two shafts with her hands. She loved the skin-like texture on the toy as she caressed their lengths. Enjoyed the aching pinch of the clamps.

"Okay, I need you to open your robe a bit more and caress the vibes across your breasts. Keep your legs wide open," Josh instructed.

Jode moved off to the side. As he watched her, his blue eyes darkened to the point where she thought she was entering a storm.

"I want you to act natural as you masturbate. Just get into it. Feel it. Live it. Love it," Jode instructed in a seductive voice. She nodded and pulled open the folds of her robe some more, freeing her breasts.

Both men inhaled sharply. Their erotic sounds sent a wicked hum through her. She glided one of the dual vibes across her nipple. Her flesh hardened. The trace of the shaft whispering along her flesh whipped exquisite shivers through her. She moved the vibe to her other nipple and caressed herself, allowing the length of one velvety hard shaft and then the other to rub her. Her eyelids grew heavy and her breathing became hitched. The camera whirred and in order to escape the naughty arousal, she forced herself to slip into her incredible high.

Jode fought for self-control. This was fucking insane. He had to stand here and watch while the woman of his dreams pleasured herself?

*Yeah, I know. It just isn't right, is it?* Josh mumbled into his mind as he kept the cameras aimed at their erotic target.

Cammie relocated the vibrator from a plump breast and lifted the toy. She parted her lips and let the tip of the cockhead slide into her mouth.

*Oh man.* Josh moaned lowly.

Jode pushed back his moan as his cock throbbed. He imagined the sensation of her lush lips enveloping his head. The pressure would be excruciatingly perfect. The hot slurp of her moist, hot tongue around his turgid flesh would be heaven. Her lips kissing his ultra-sensitive length. Her tongue lapping and loving his shaft just as she was doing now to the toy.

*I'd appreciate it if you toned your imagination down a bit, brother. I don't know how long I can hold on with you daydreaming about her. I have enough fantasies of my own,* Josh grumbled.

Jode cursed as Josh's arousal pulsed into his system.

Fuck, could this get any worse?

Josh grimaced at the pressure distressing his cock and balls. He thought he would be able to handle watching her and taking photos, but he could barely keep his attention to his equipment. The shots of her making love to the toy were provocative, searing and sensational. She was a natural in front of the camera, acting as if they weren't even here.

His fingers trembled as he played with the timers. His body shuddered as he whispered to Jode to get out of his clothes so they could get on with the next phase of the shoot, which would be the two of them watching her masturbate.

He didn't have a clue how he'd be able to stand not joining in with her on her toy fuck-fest.

Cammie could hear them breathing. They were close but she dared not open her eyes. This next scene was a part of the shoot. Her masturbating while they watched.

Oh boy, what had she gotten herself into? She should have halted this erotic insanity the moment those two men said it would only be the three of them. Why hadn't she taken the initiative and called Sex Toys for confirmation? Why weren't the owners here? Alison had said they had been eager to meet her.

Why was she even questioning this? The three of them were working out perfectly together. Too perfectly.

"Okay, open your eyes, Cammie. We want you looking at us while you masturbate," Josh coached.

Oh no. Not good.

"Don't be shy," Jode prodded. "It needs to look stimulating for the potential customers. We want them buying our products."

*Yes. I must stay focused. Stay professional, girl.*

She was being silly with her arousal. She could handle this. But tonight when they left, she would have one hell of a masturbating session.

Cammie blinked her eyes open and totally forgot how to caress her toy.

*Oh. Wow.*

Both men stood nearby. Lush and naked. And very aroused.

Their cocks were unbelievably long and large. She couldn't take her eyes off them. Couldn't even remember how to breathe.

They were stroking themselves. Their eyes appeared heavy-lidded and their fingers trailed along their massive lengths slowly and teasingly. She began to shake with need. She wanted to touch them and taste them. She wanted to fuck them.

"That's the dreamy, sensual look we want. Go with it, Cammie," Josh encouraged.

She was not being the skilled model by staring at them with need. This craving to touch their erections went way beyond what she was accustomed to in this line of work. She was unbelievably excited and poised on the edge of some wicked high she'd never encountered before. Instincts told her that tumbling over the precipice would be euphoric and highly satisfying.

Every part of her hurt as she fought to stop thinking and feeling this wonderful arousal over two guys she didn't even know. Truth was, she couldn't imagine finding two hotter, sexier men for this shoot. Or for herself.

• • ❧ • •

"OKAY, CAMMIE. LET'S take a break and look at the pictures and video. Then you can sign off on the ones we all agree on," Josh instructed.

*Are you fucking insane? You want to do business now?* Jode's desperate voice echoed in Josh's mind. His brother's torment had seeped deep inside Josh and he swore they were both hanging by a thread of self-control.

*I'll take her right there on that bed now if we don't stop*, he warned Jode.

*Then we'll take her.*

*No, not this way. She needs to get to know us better.*

If she had been any other woman, Josh knew he just might have stepped over the line and fucked his brains out with her. He could tell Cammie desired to have sex too. She was attracted to both of them. It was in the sultry way she gazed at them as they stroked their cocks. It was in the glistening wetness between her thighs. There was a chemistry between them. She needed them.

*Fuck, you have the restraints of a monk.*

Josh chuckled at his brother's comment.

*Nice, Jode. Nice. Now let's show the woman some respect and stop this before it gets out of hand. We've got plenty of time to get her to fall in love with us.*

Jode cursed, bent over and grabbed his pants. Josh did the same but he caught peeks of disappointment and confusion whispering over Cammie's face.

Heck, they really should tell her the truth. But they were in too deep now. If they told her about the stupid bet, then she'd most likely give them the boot and Earl would get Sexy Toys. Personally he'd rather have Cammie know what was going on. To hell with the company. But seeing that arrogant smirk on Earl's face vanish when they delivered before the deadline would be beneficial to all of them in the long run. That bastard needed to be wiped out from the company. Most of all, Earl needed to be taught a lesson for whatever he'd done to Cammie.

• • ⚓ • •

"WOW, THESE PICTURES all look fantastic," Cammie whispered in awe as she sat with Josh's laptop in front of her on top of the kitchen table.

"Hard to pick which ones are the best, isn't it?" Josh said around a mouthful of steak.

Both men had been thrilled to learn food was available to them when the doorbell had rung and the deliveryman presented the items she'd ordered from a takeout restaurant in a nearby town. Both men possessed wonderful appetites. She could easily picture herself cooking for them. Something delicious like lamb, baby potatoes and creamy spinach. She loved cooking and people always said a way to a man's heart was through his stomach.

Cammie blinked at that thought. Gosh, she was being pathetic daydreaming about two complete strangers. She needed to snap out of this infatuation with them.

"I seriously didn't know you were such a good photographer, bro," Jode replied, as he forked coleslaw into his mouth.

The food had arrived shortly after they'd ended the photo session. Thankfully, dinner had been the distraction they all needed. But the sexual tension did continue to hang in the air between them, mainly because of the provocative photos flashing across the laptop screen.

She swore she'd never looked so...sultry and needy, in photos. Either Jode was right and Josh was a very talented photographer, or her erotic look had something to do with being sexually attracted to these two younger men.

*Cougar.* That word burst into her mind like a lightning bolt. Was it possible she was into much younger men? Was that why she'd never been overly attracted to men who were closer to her age? Would she not have noticed this interesting characteristic earlier in her life?

Cammie rolled her eyes and bit her bottom lip in denial. Nope, it had to be these two men and nothing to do with age. Her mother once told her some women just knew instinctively when a man would be the right one. Unfortunately her mother had never mentioned Cammie might fall for two guys. How would she ever explain such an attraction to her family?

*Oh brother.* Nothing had happened between the three of them and nothing was going to happen. Those men were just a couple of studs who were scrumptious eye candy and nothing more. So why did she believe it was more than that?

"Why does Sexy Toys have such a short deadline?" Cammie blurted.

That question had been nagging her and now that she was able to gather her thoughts, things about this photo shoot just didn't sit right. Getting an answer regarding the timeline would most likely answer everything.

Both men froze.

*Hmm, interesting reaction.*

"If you would please keep this information under your hat, Cammie, we would appreciate it. The new owners realize that the company needs a boost in sales immediately or the company may face bankruptcy down the line," Josh said quickly.

"Oh, I hadn't realized." An arrow of desperation to save the company zipped through her.

"But rest assured the possibility is small and you will still get paid for your services. The advance will clear. No need to worry on that. Sexy Toys will take good care of their number-one star. We realize that you are the most likely person who can save Sexy Toys."

"No pressure intended," Jode chimed in.

Both men did appear apprehensive. More worried than a couple of very hot-looking male models should be. They were so sexy other companies would snap them up if Sexy Toys went under. Heck, they must have offers coming out of their ears, especially with their, um...sizes.

"When you were with the company, sales went through the roof. So the owners decided to move on this idea of hiring you as quickly as possible," Josh said.

"But the deadline is by this Friday?" she prodded. It just didn't make sense.

"The new owners are young and spur-of-the-moment," Jode rushed to say.

"Yes, very spontaneous," Josh said with a smile. "They do their best work with unplanned events. Believe us, we know."

"When do I get to meet them?"

Both men looked at each other as if they had no idea how to answer her question.

"They want to meet you. Badly," Josh replied.

Jode nodded in agreement.

"But?" she nudged.

"They're busy," Jode said with a bit too much eagerness.

"Yes, very busy. Something suddenly came up and they had to attend to other business out of town. But you'll get to meet them."

"When?" My, they certainly did seem nervous, didn't they?

"Friday. You'll meet them Friday if you want to come to the presentation. We can introduce you. And they will love everything. They will love you, Cammie," Josh said softly.

"Just as much as we do," Jode added.

"Such sweet compliments will get you nowhere," she kidded.

She would give Alison a call tonight and update her about the company and potential bankruptcy. She hoped Alison wouldn't advise her to pull out of this gig, because she wanted to get to know more about these two men. So much more.

• • ⌘ • •

"WE SHOULD HAVE STAYED," Jode complained as Josh steered the van off Cammie's secluded driveway onto a local road.

"Sure, and how did you propose we stay? Ask her if we could spend the night?" Josh snapped. There was a hard edge to his brother's voice. One of desperation and need for release. It whipped through Jode as well but so far he'd managed to keep himself under control, although barely.

"Why not? It would be a great excuse to get an early start in the morning."

"And have her hearing us masturbating? No thanks. I'd rather do that in the hotel shower. My release is going to be a killer by the hard-on I have."

Jode grinned. "She's quite the woman, isn't she? She's smart, has a sense of humor and she's attracted to both of us. I've never felt so alive. It's tenfold to when I saw her in those photos on the conference walls. It's so weird falling for a girl in a picture, isn't it?"

Josh smiled and nodded as he kept his eyes glued to the road.

Jode resisted the urge to shuffle his butt around on his seat due to his arousal discomfort. Moving just might be the stimulation he needed to come, and this was not a good place for release. He'd prefer to reach satisfaction in the shower or his hotel bed or, better yet, with Cammie.

"We just need to make sure she doesn't get in touch with anyone at the company or they'll blow our cover," Josh pondered.

"I've already taken care of that," Jode replied. "After dinner when I went to the bathroom, I gave Kim a call on my cell and told her that if anyone, including Cammie, calls asking for us we are out of town until Friday. Thankfully, she didn't ask questions and she assured me she would let reception know. If Cammie calls Sexy Toys, that's the message she'll get."

"At least we are out of town. That part is true."

"I can tell you I just about collapsed when Cammie said she wanted a meeting with us." Jode chuckled.

"You and me both. I thought it was all over. I figured we'd spill the truth and she'd send us packing and we would never see her again."

"Instead, we have a date to continue with the shoot first thing in the morning," Jode replied.

"I can't wait," Josh whispered and Jode noticed his brother's hands tighten on the steering wheel.

Waiting was going to be such a bitch for both of them.

# Chapter Four

CAMMIE BLEW OUT A TENSE breath and tossed her cell phone onto the bathroom countertop. She'd tried to call Alison several times over the past half hour while she'd tidied up the kitchen, but her calls had gone straight to Alison's voice mail.

For a fleeting moment she thought about contacting Kim, a friend of hers who'd worked for Sexy Toys. Maybe Kim would have some more news about these two male models. But she'd lost touch with everyone at the company and didn't want to rekindle any friendships at this time. She dropped the idea and gazed at herself in the mirror.

Her cheeks were flushed and her eyes were bright with eagerness. She'd never felt so alive before. Her body tingled with need. Her pussy was sopping wet and her breasts felt swollen and her nipples were extremely tender.

She even felt happy.

This was crazy. Wonderfully crazy, to be thinking about Josh and Jode and wanting them in her bed making mad passionate love to her. She shouldn't have let them go tonight. They'd mentioned they were staying at a hotel in the nearby town. She should have asked them to spend the night here. Yes, both of them.

She shook her head as a mad giggle erupted between her lips. Could she really sleep with two guys at the same time? Cammie reached up and held her hot cheeks. Did those two even do that sort of thing? Maybe she'd ask them to stay over tomorrow night.

*Oh my gosh.* No, she couldn't do such a thing. The pleasure created in the photo shoots was just part of the job. No, she couldn't be with them, although she wanted to. They were so much younger. She would just have to satisfy herself the old-fashioned way.

Masturbating.

Better yet, masturbating with one of those toys situated in the cartons. Cammie bit her bottom lip as she strolled into the living room. The sun had just dipped behind the horizon, casting the room into semi-darkness. The cameras and other equipment were still set up near the nook, an indication she hadn't dreamed up today. The sexy twins had truly been here.

After switching on the lights, she rummaged through one of the already-opened boxes. She located a couple of remote-controlled heart-shaped egg vibrators, matching nipple vibrator clamps and some lube. Would they notice that the packages had been opened? She could mention she'd been curious...or she could tell them the truth. That she'd used the toys while fantasizing about them.

Oh, she'd come up with some excuse when the time came. Right now she wanted some heavy-duty sexual release. She shivered with anticipation as she made her way around her home making sure all her doors and windows were locked. Then she shut off the lights and headed upstairs with her toys, where she quickly cleaned the items with soapy water in the upstairs bathroom.

She eyed the bathtub. Should she take a shower first? No, she'd waited long enough. Hanging her robe onto the hook on her bathroom door, she gripped the lube and squirted some onto her middle finger. The lube was cool and creamy and her anus clenched and gripped around her finger as she pushed past her sphincter and probed inside. She withdrew, applied some more lube and continued until she was generously lubricated.

After washing her hands thoroughly with soap and water, she grabbed her toys, the lube and some hand cleanser. Then, leaving the bathroom lights on, she stepped into her adjoining bedroom. This was the largest room in the house. It was her sanctuary. Her domain.

The bathroom lights splashed just enough brightness into her room that she could see everything. She'd spared no expense decorating her room in her favorite colors—several shades of white and pink.

Dainty pale-pink lace curtains with scalloped edges hung on her two large windows. From a local Amish handyman, she'd purchased a hand-carved cherrywood king-sized canopied bed and matching furniture. The princess canopy was white lace, luxuriously draped over the top and spilled down the sides of her bed like a white waterfall, making her feel as if she were enveloped in the safety and privacy of a cocoon while she slept.

Despite floral wallpaper not being the "in" thing these days, she'd defied modern and papered two of her walls with traditional quaint red-rose floral wallpaper and two walls with lush pink paint.

Her floor was wide-planked cherrywood and she'd placed several throw rugs with cheerful white-and-rose-colored themes on the floor throughout her room. It was a very feminine bedroom, the kind her childhood friends had and one she'd always craved to have when she'd been a kid, but her family had been very poor. She'd had to share one very small room stuffed with two wobbly metal bunk beds along with three loud younger sisters who didn't give her any privacy.

But now was not the time to dwell on her past or admire her room. It was time for serious business. Settling the toys onto the nightstand, she whipped aside the plush white quilt and slipped between the welcome coolness of her pink satin sheets.

Reaching out, she grabbed the toys and placed the items onto the bed beside her. She took a deep shuddering breath and lay on her side facing her assortment. After she picked up one of the dual heart-shaped vibrating eggs, she lubed it and gently inserted it into her lubricated anus, pushing it in nice and deep.

When the time came to remove it, all she would have to do was pull on the plastic wire string that was attached to both eggs. She followed up by scrubbing her fingers with some alcohol hand cleanser. Then she turned onto her back. Lifting her knees, she spread her thighs and inserted the other egg into her moist vagina.

Next she massaged her fingers over her nipples, shuddering at the exquisite sensations as she tweaked and pulled and twisted until they were hard, red and wonderfully achy. Then she pinched the two nipple clamps onto her tender flesh, gasping at the pleasure-pain they created.

She located the remote control and pressed the button until the desired wicked vibrating pulsed through her ass from the vibrating egg. A moment later, the other egg came to life, pulsing inside her vagina. She moaned softly at the unbelievably erotic sensations they created. A moment later she had both clamps pulsating at her nipples.

With one hand she massaged first one breast and then the other, rubbing around her areolas, careful not to disturb the clamps. Using her other hand, she dipped her fingers between her thighs and moaned softly as she touched her sensitive clit.

Mercy, but she was creaming up a storm. She pushed a finger past her plump pussy lips and gathered some moisture from her vagina. Using her juices as lube, she briskly rubbed her clit with a gentle yet firm pressure to create the stirrings of a climax.

She imagined Jode and Josh climbing onto the bed on each side of her. Their hands roving over her breasts and their fingers tweaking her nipples as much as the clamps were doing now.

Need surged through her.

Panting, she massaged her clit harder and faster, moaning as she imagined Jode and Josh grabbing her, their firm fingers clutching her arms as they held her captive.

*Oh my gosh.*

Their lusty blue gazes made love to her. One of them kissed her. His dominating lips pressed fiercely against hers. The other man rubbed her clit with his cockhead.

*Yes. Harder.*

Every nerve in her body vibrated. Heat whipped through her. She massaged her clit quicker and rougher. The egg vibes trembled inside her pussy and ass. Pleasure-pain coursed into her clamped nipples. She imagined their mouths sucking on her nipples, tasting her and loving her.

She fantasized about Jode thrusting his cock into her vagina. Her legs trembled and she bore down, tightening her thighs as she continued massaging her clit with a desperate fierceness. Lifting her hand from her left breast, she drove her thumb in and and out of her mouth, imagining Jode's swollen head sinking in and out of her mouth.

*Yes. Perfect.*

She finger-fucked her mouth with a wicked desperation and stroked her clit with incredible speed. An erotic hum whispered over her. She slipped into the high and molten ecstasy as it rolled over her, swallowed her and carried her along an avenue of quivering convulsions and shuddering desire.

She exploded on a strangled moan. She gyrated her hips, gasping with shock as the intense climax scattered her senses and ripped through her body and mind like a magnificent storm. She became lost and rode the waves.

Nothing mattered. Just the unbelievable, shattering pleasure. When it finally subsided, she was left in a world of dazed surprise and intoxicating shock.

*Wow. That was magnificent.*

She could only imagine how incredible the real thing would be.

• • ⤳ • •

AS THE SHOTS OF WATER from the showerhead sprayed his rigid cock, Josh fought for control. He imagined grabbing Cammie by her shoulders, pushing her down onto her knees in front of him. Then he'd thrust his cock into her succulent mouth.

She'd moan her acceptance of his immense size and her warm lips would envelop his shaft. Her tongue would slurp along his shaft and she'd use her teeth to nibble his tender flesh, creating just the perfect sparks of pleasure-pain that he required to orgasm.

His thighs tightened. He rubbed more soap along his shaft and balls, then massaged his scrotum, imagining how dark Cammie's eyes would be as she looked up at him.

Lust would shine there. Need and want for him.

*Man, what the hell are doing? You are killing me.* Jode's words crashed into Josh like a boulder.

*C'mon! What do you think I'm doing? Do you mind giving me some privacy?*

*Not when you're wrapping me up so damned tight I may not even come.*

*Ouch. That must be painful.* Josh snickered and continued stroking himself.

He tensed as erotic tingles not created by his fingers whispered along the length of his shaft.

*Fuck!* He could now feel Jode's pulsing arousal along with his.

*Sorry, brother. It looks as if we're in this together,* Jode said.

*For once, just once, I thought I could just be alone with my imagination and Cammie.*

*Dream on, brother. Dream on. You know you love it.*

Jode grinned as Josh cursed into his mind. But he knew Josh wasn't seriously mad. They'd come to accept their intimate problem a long time ago. Josh was frustrated, that was all. Just as irritated as Jode. They should have found a way to get an invitation into Cammie's bed.

*Too late for should-haves,* Josh warned.

Jode's shaft tightened as Josh's arousal pulsed in rhythm with his own.

*Hell, you couldn't have waited until I had gotten into my own shower?*

No response. That meant only one thing.

Jode quickly dropped his pants and underwear, allowing his tortured flesh to be free. Quickly, he lay on the bed. Blowing out a tense breath, he kneaded his aching balls with one hand and roughly stroked the length of his erection with his other hand.

Cammie's vision burst into his mind. Her, leaning over him. Her dark hair trailing over her shoulders, hiding her breasts from him. Her smile was wide with appreciation as she stared down at his cock. Heat embraced him as she parted her lips and accepted his cockhead into her succulent mouth.

*Man! This feels good!*

*Oh, Cammie,* Jode whispered.

Josh echoed his brother's thoughts by calling her name too. He struggled to breathe and groaned as the pressure continued to build. He could almost feel the pressure of her lips melt around his flesh. Could feel the tickle of her hair as it whispered over his trembling thighs.

His hands worked his swollen flesh faster.

*She's so beautiful. Can you see her from my mind?* he whispered to Josh.

*Yes,* came his tortured voice from somewhere far away.

Jode's shaft throbbed right along with Josh's, pulsing beneath his fingers. Perspiration whispered across his brow.

Cammie sucked hard and Jode exploded on a strangled shout, his body racked by spasms. A split second later he heard Josh shout Cammie's name and they both came together.

• • ഹ • •

"WE CAN START IN THE upstairs bathroom this morning. Your agent said it would be perfect for the water toys," Josh said as he watched Cammie's curvy butt wiggle sexily against her tight blue jeans as she walked toward the kitchen after welcoming him and his brother into her home.

She'd been bubbly upon opening the door. Her eyes twinkled with happiness and her cheeks flushed a pretty pink when she saw them. She'd been cheerful, talking up a storm, not letting them get in a word edgewise. Josh was beginning to understand that she talked a lot when she was nervous and that's how they'd ended up in the situation of her mistaking them as the models.

She'd also seemed a bit shy this morning. He wondered what was up with that. Especially because after greeting them and bringing them inside she'd rushed off toward the kitchen, insisting that they all have some coffee before starting their day of shooting.

Before coming over, Josh and Jode had had their morning coffee after their run, and he'd thought they could get to work right away. But if she required them to join her for breakfast, hell, he would do whatever she wanted.

*She looks fantastic, doesn't she?* Jode whispered into his mind as they walked toward the camera equipment where they'd left it yesterday.

*She looks hot and aroused. I bet if I dipped my finger into her vagina she'd be wet and needy.*

*Oh man, why are you doing this to me?* Jode groaned, shook his head and glared angrily at him.

*Payback for last night in not allowing me to get into the shower before you started fantasizing about her. Now shut up and help me get the camera and toys upstairs.*

They needed to hurry. He'd dreamed about Cammie all night. Scorching dreams of her breasts jiggling up and down as she rode him into hundreds of orgasms while they'd been soaking in a bathtub full of bubbles. He hoped to make that dream come true today. He'd awoken with a very painful hard-on. Masturbating in the shower before their run had taken the edge off, but he wasn't sure if he could even handle what he'd planned for them today. Especially if he'd read her wrong yesterday about her being attracted to them.

*I don't remember Alison mentioning Cammie's upstairs bathroom?*

*She didn't,* Josh said truthfully.

*Then why...*

*It's one step closer to her bedroom.*

Jode chuckled out loud and Josh threw him a shut-the-fuck-up look.

*She doesn't read our minds, remember?*

Josh ignored his reminder.

"You wouldn't by chance have some bubble bath, would you?" he called out to Cammie.

She appeared in the doorway and his breath backed up into his lungs at the sight of her standing there with that shy look of hers. The cute way she avoided their gazes and the sweet way she nibbled on her lower lip as she thought just about made him come on the spot.

That provocative blouse she wore spoke to him. It was a simple, virginal white filmy type of garment. Damned sexy in that he could make out shadowy outlines of her areolas as well as her bold nipples pressing proudly against the material. It made him wonder what was going on in that pretty little head of hers to wear a teasing top like that.

"Yes, I do. Several different types. I love taking baths. You'll find all the bottles right on the countertop. Help yourself to anything you need for the shoot. Coffee will be done in just a few minutes, so be back soon. And I've also got some fruit and croissants."

She disappeared.

*Yesterday, she fed us dinner. This morning she wants to give us breakfast. She's eager to take care of us,* Jode said as he strolled toward the stairs with some of the equipment.

*Let's hope she'll take care of us in more ways than just breakfast,* Josh answered.

He tried to ignore the throbbing of his cock and balls as well as his brother's growing sexual discomfort at seeing Cammie. He picked up an open carton of toys and followed Jode.

$$\cdot\cdot\text{❧}\cdot\cdot$$

CAMMIE STARED AT THE coffeemaker and silently urged it to hurry up. She needed coffee to calm herself. She'd been dumb in not having a cup or two or three after returning from her early-morning run. But she'd slept in this morning thanks to being awake half the night masturbating some more after dreaming about having sex with those two hunky twins. When she'd returned from her run she'd showered and changed and had just put on some light makeup when the doorbell had rung.

Seeing them again...she'd forgotten how tall the two men were and how enticing they smelled. This morning, it seemed as if their scents of aftershave and fresh soap affected her even more than she remembered. Her legs were trembling, her heart was racing and her mind wouldn't stop giving her images of both men touching her intimately.

Boy oh boy, she was in trouble. Last night's vow to stick to masturbating where they were concerned was going out the window. She was changing her mind. She wanted them in her bed. Being near them, seeing the lust flaring in their eyes as they'd gazed at her when she'd opened the door, had her heart fluttering, her pussy quivering and her racing for that comfort food of coffee. The dark-roasted scent wafted through the air, teasing her nostrils, bringing her back to reality. Why did she suddenly get the feeling coffee was not going help calm her down this time?

• • ᴖᴕᴏ • •

JODE'S COCK AND BALLS were harder and more swollen than yesterday as he inhaled her scent. It floated everywhere. It was in the air. On the bubble bath containers. On the towels. And on the soft robe he'd caressed and smelled as it hung on a nearby hook.

He should masturbate right here and now in this bathroom. He could get off quickly before he went back downstairs for that coffee she was so gung-ho on giving them. But making himself flaccid would defeat the purpose of seducing her, wouldn't it? His shaft needed to be hard and swollen for the shots Josh would be taking of them. He just hoped she would forgive them for not setting her straight about them not being the models. Starting a relationship on a lie was not good. If they just confessed to her about the bet and who they were, she would forgive them. Wouldn't she?

*Stop thinking about our lies and concentrate on getting the bathtub looking right.*

Jode frowned and turned to find Josh standing in the bathroom doorway with more photography equipment.

"We should wait until after breakfast before running the hot water into the tub. I don't want her getting into cold water," Jode said as he moved to the box containing the toys. He withdrew some of the ones they were going to use.

"An ice-cold shower is what I need and you'll run the water now. It can't be too hot or it'll steam up my lens," Josh growled. His eyes flashed with irritation.

*The man is moody,* Jode teased.

Josh gave him the middle finger, then stepped into the bathroom and began setting up the cameras and lighting.

Jode started the water running, making sure it wasn't too hot or too mild. *Screw Josh.*

*I heard that.*

Jode chuckled and moved to the open box of toys.

"A couple of these have already been opened," Jode mused as he withdrew the packages containing the heart-shaped egg vibrators and matching nipple clamps. The scent of soap drifted beneath his nostrils.

*What the...?*

*What?*

*She used a couple of these toys last night.* Jode grinned.

*Only a couple?* Amusement etched Josh's voice as he came to stand beside Jode and gazed at the toys.

*It looks like it.*

*I'm insulted. I would have thought she'd have used all the toys in her desperation to get us off her mind.*

Jode threw his brother a sideways glance. *Funny. Ha ha.*

Josh laughed and returned to fiddling with his cameras.

*Should we say something to her about it?* Jode pondered as he replaced the items back into the box and removed some others.

*Why? So you can embarrass her? Let me handle this. We want her comfortable with us,* Josh replied.

*Comfortable is not the word I would use. Needy. Sexy. Craving us as much as we are wanting her are better words.*

*Okay. Okay, needy. We'll get her needy with this next shoot, I promise.*

Jode nodded. He could hardly wait!

. . ❧ . .

CAMMIE WAS WORKING on finishing her second cup of hot black coffee in the kitchen when the two men descended the stairs. Despite not wanting to, she tensed at their approaching footsteps. When they walked into the room, her breath halted as she surveyed how truly wide their shoulders were and how they towered over her. Suddenly the kitchen seemed much smaller and much cozier with them in it.

"So how did you sleep last night?" Josh asked as he pulled out a chair at the table and sat down.

Cammie just about gulped her coffee the wrong way at that question. His gaze was intense as he studied her for an answer. Or maybe he was looking for a reaction? Had they already noticed a couple of the toy packages had been opened?

Oh dear, she still hadn't figured out a way to explain it.

"Fine and you two?"

"Great," Josh and Jode said rather quickly. They both reached for their coffees and began sipping at the same time.

It was an odd experience seeing identical twins sitting at her breakfast table. Kind of like seeing double.

*Double trouble,* an inner voice reminded her. *Keep your mind on your job and you will be fine. Not.*

They'd both brushed their hair back off their foreheads today and wore dark shadows of beard stubble on their faces, which gave them an allure of danger and sexiness. The rush of blood pulsed through her just knowing she would be working intimately with these two men again today.

She could tell them apart now too without the need for them to smile so she could see which side the dimples appeared in their cheeks. She'd realized that Josh's nose was a bit wider and longer than Jode's nose. And Jode's chin had a bit of cleft in the middle, where Josh's was less pronounced. They'd dressed in jeans and black polo shirts that caressed their well-defined muscles. Just looking at them made beautiful butterflies shiver in her lower belly.

"The bathroom is nice. Absolutely spot-on for the next shoot. Did you decorate it yourself?" Jode asked.

Cammie blinked in surprise and realized she'd been staring at them. Heat fused into her cheeks as she nodded. "I decorated the entire house."

"You have good taste," Jode complimented her.

*Good taste in younger men too,* that naughty inner voice of hers whispered.

"Thank you." Her cheeks were getting hotter.

Both men grinned.

"You don't seem to be used to compliments. You're blushing," Josh said softly.

*Oh great! Floor, please part and take me away.*

"Would you like something with your coffee? Some fruit? Croissants?" She lifted a bowl laden with fresh drizzled chocolate mini-croissants nestled in an arrangement of fresh ripe strawberries and mango slices. She'd picked everything up on the way back from her run from a neighboring bakery and bed-and-breakfast a quarter mile up the lake road. It had been a bitch trying to keep everything from getting too shaken as she'd run but the owner, Joyce, had been kind enough to pack everything tightly in containers and thankfully the fruit and croissants had survived with minimum damage.

Both men nodded and eagerly grabbed one of each, placing them in the plates she'd set.

"You can have more. I have plenty," she urged.

Both men grinned and reached for more helpings.

She wanted to see them devour food as they'd done last night. It made her content to see them eat and to know she was supplying food they enjoyed. She inhaled softly at those thoughts. Heavens, was she trying to domesticate them already?

Extreme happiness slipped into her as the men dug into their food.

"Now that's more like it." She laughed.

As they ate they discussed the weather, the men's love of playing golf and to her surprise, their shared love of running.

When she told them she also ran they didn't appear surprised at all and when she revealed she'd never played golf before, their eager offers of teaching her the sport had her so excited she couldn't think straight. By the time the meal was finished, she'd been talked into joining them tomorrow morning for a run around the lake she lived on and when the photo shoot was finished she had a promise from them that they would teach her how to play golf.

"I think we'd better get some work done or we'll be too full to do anything today." Jode stared at his empty plate, leaned back in his chair and patted his ultra-flat belly.

"I'm surprised you were able to stuff all that food into you, brother." Josh laughed as he stood.

"For energy, my man. We're going to need it today," he replied. He gazed at Cammie and winked.

She trembled with excitement. Why did she get the feeling they were talking about more than just the photo shoot?

# Chapter Five

IN HER BEDROOM SHE undressed to just a pair of panties, as instructed by Josh. Then she slipped into her robe, inhaled deeply and entered the adjoining bathroom. It was crowded in here with the equipment and props. But the lighting seemed perfect.

Vanilla scented the room and soft sunlight splashed through the lone window onto the tub filled with kaleidoscope-colored bubbles. Tiny flames flickered from an arrangement of vanilla candles lined along the bathtub rim. Also settled upon the rim were bright-red toys they wanted to use during this scene.

Both men stood beside the cameras, appearing eager to get started.

"Jode set it up. What do you think?" Josh asked.

*I think I want to jump into the tub and have wild hot sex with the both of you*, Cammie pondered. She quickly pushed aside those thoughts.

*Focus on the job, woman.*

"It looks seductive," she admitted.

"Seductive will have to do." Jode chuckled. His eyes appeared glazed with anticipation as he looked at the arrangement of toys.

Both men had also changed into their robes and at the thought of climbing into the tub with them, heat sped through her like wildfire.

"Cammie, you'll have to wear these nipple clamps."

*Oh my!*

She tensed as Josh handed her a cute pair with tiny dolphins and miniature hearts dangling.

"As soon as I check if everything is okay with the cameras I'll join you. Cammie in the middle, please."

Cammie nodded jerkily and swallowed as her mouth went dry.

*Oh my gosh.* She hadn't been this nervous since her first few nude toy insert photo shoots. She averted their eyes as she slipped out of the robe and hung it back onto the hook where she'd retrieved it earlier. Jode also removed his robe. He held out his hand and his fingers were hot against hers as she accepted his help in getting into the tub. Strength powered through his palm and he held her steady. Soft bubbles and warm water tickled her feet and her breath halted momentarily as she imagined the heat of their gazes on her back.

After turning around, she sat and the bubbles came to just below her nipples. Jode stepped into the tub, giving her a sexy view of his very engorged long, swollen shaft and balls.

*Wow, he's so well hung.* Not that he wasn't yesterday, but today it seemed as if he was seriously erect. His shaft, aiming up toward his belly, was shaded purplish and woven with bulging veins and a mushroom-shaped cockhead.

Searing heat wafted from his body as he sat down right next to her. His thigh pressed intimately against hers and her breaths erupted in sweet-sounding gasps that she'd never heard before in her life.

He grinned at her, but it was a tight, aroused smile. Bronze-tanned muscles laced his sinewy shoulders and a thick mat of brown curly hair covered his wide chest.

She pictured herself straddling him. Guiding his cock into her cunt.

Josh cleared his throat and ripped Cammie back to reality.

"Nipple clamps," Josh reminded her. "And we need your nipples plumped too to make them look bigger and darker for the camera."

Today she didn't feel as daring as yesterday in asking them to put the clamps on. Jode's erotic touches as he'd rubbed her pussy lips had put her on the sexual edge. Her nipples had always been the most tender of her erogenous zones, and she didn't know how she would react having Jode touching her there.

"Would you like me to put the clamps on? I have some gel here to help plump your nipples," Jode asked softly.

*Oh my goodness.* She couldn't stop the sweet shivers as sexual awareness dashed through her.

His eyes glittered as he studied her and awaited an answer.

"Sure," she whispered.

She cast a glance at Josh and her tummy fluttered. He was watching them with penetrating interest.

"Here goes," Jode whispered.

She could barely suppress a moan when Jode's hot hand tenderly—and to her surprise, possessively—cupped her breast. As he held her, he dabbed a generous amount of gel onto her left nipple with the fingers of his other hand. Her flesh immediately tingled.

He massaged and pinched her nipple until carnal shudders arrowed right down between her thighs. Involuntarily she arched her back, pushing her breasts outward.

"Hold that look, Cammie." Josh's voice curled over her like an aphrodisiac.

Cammie breathed into the arousal. There was something truly sexy in the way Jode held her breast. As if he were handling something valuable. As if he wanted to show her how much he desired her.

She almost laughed out loud at her silly thoughts. She was reading way too much into her reactions to him. It was just a photo shoot. But he did feel so good in the erotic manner his thigh rubbed ever so softly against hers.

The camera whirred, taking photos of them. In her mind's eye she could imagine how carnal the pictures were going to appear when they studied them later. She inhaled sharply as Jode gave her nipple a few pinches. Pricks of sweet pain had her gasping.

She didn't realize that Josh had stepped into the tub with them—actually behind her—until he instructed her to move a bit forward so he could scoot in and sit behind her.

Wow, if ever she'd been smart to order an extra-large bathtub, this time was it. His body heat radiated against her backside and she inhaled at his hard-as-nails cock pressing against the crack in her buttocks. Too bad she wore that panty. She bit back a moan as she envisioned him sliding his swollen shaft deep into her ass.

Jode said nothing as he continued tending to her breast but the erotic tension hung so heavy in the air she swore she could slice it with a knife.

Water sloshed and tinkled as Josh slipped a bent leg against each side of her hips. Mesmerized by their nearness, she watched Josh's hand snake around and she couldn't hold back a whimper as he cupped her other breast. He began kneading her nipple in much the same way as Jode. She panted as his cockhead throbbed against her flesh and his thighs cradled her hips with possession.

Wow. Here she was with two hotties in a tub full of bubbles. How cool was that going to look on the company's website?

"This is picture-perfect, Cammie," Josh whispered into her ear. "Just keep your eyes closed and save that sultry look while we place the clamps. And then we'll go into the next phase of the shoot."

Cammie could barely nod as her body tightened with excitement. What was the next phase? She should have asked for an outline before starting today's photo shoot. But she'd been too excited to get on with it. How long could she hold out without orgasming right here? She could scarcely restrain herself from dipping her fingers beneath the bubbles to find her clit and massaging herself into climax. Her pussy lips felt swollen, her clit needy for a rough massage.

The cameras continued taking pictures. This time she didn't fall into the usual high that she experienced during shoots. This time a hum of wicked want whispered through her body. She needed more from them. Wanted so much more of the caring way they caressed her nipples.

The pressure of their fingers playing with her nipples made her moan and gasp. The sound was animalistic and erotic and she wondered what Jode and Josh were thinking. Did they realize how much their touches were turning her on? Or was this just all part of the job for them?

Her insides melted when Josh let go of her breast and cupped her chin. His fingers continued tweaking her nipples while he angled her head toward him. It was an awkward position and she fully expected to get a kink in her neck. But nothing happened. Instead, the firm, warm pressure of his mouth heated over her lips.

Her brain almost short-circuited and she struggled to regain composure. Sexual hunger roared inside her.

*It's just part of the shoot,* an inner voice urged. *Nothing more.*

Oh, she wanted to kiss him back so badly. Wanted this to be more than just a show for the cameras. His lips caressed hers so intimately, her body jerked. He groaned an untamed and erotic noise that sent desirable shock waves coursing through her.

Jode touched her bare shoulder with his moist lips. He trailed feather-light kisses across her collarbone while Josh continued possessing her mouth. Somewhere deep in her mind, a voice warned her, these kisses and touches went deeper than mere show. They wanted her, and she knew she wouldn't protest if they took her right here in the tub.

• • ᴄᴧ◦ • •

*SHE IS A PERFECT FIT,* Josh muttered into Jode's mind but Jode could barely hear him as Cammie's sweet whimpers held most of his attention. The rest was centered in his engorged cock, which begged for immediate attention.

*Her nipples are quite sensitive. She's really enjoying this,* Josh continued.

Jode wanted to tell his brother to shut the fuck up, but he couldn't break the magnetic hold Cammie had over his senses. She was killing him. Her sweetly parted lips were so damned inviting he was hanging by a single thread of self-control and any second he just knew he was going to lose it.

*Clamp her nipples and let's get on with the shoot,* Josh ordered. Jode sensed his brother's intense need as it pounded through him and added to his torment.

He didn't want this to end. He loved her sexual sounds. He loved her. How could it be possible that the more he knew her, the more he wanted to know about her? He'd never experienced this phenomenon with any other woman he'd bedded.

*Josh was right. She is perfect. She is the one for us.*

Frustration and annoyance whipped through Josh. He wanted Jode to get on with the clamping of her nipples but nothing happened. Josh understood why not. He was having a hell of a hard time letting go of Cammie's nipple himself. There was no way he could hold out through listening to her musical mews, though. Every time she gasped, every time she inhaled, his entire being shuddered. It was as if she were a part of him now. He could barely hear Jode's thoughts. But Jode's needs continued to spiral through Josh, increasing the urgency to make love to her.

He cursed himself for instructing Cammie to put on her panties. That thin piece of material was the only thing that kept him from spearing his aching cock deep into her ass. Maybe he should just rip it off her body?

He trembled at that thought. Shivered at the idea of how wild the pressure of her anal muscles wrapping around his swollen shaft would feel.

"Take me," she whispered. Her voice was so low that he wasn't even sure if he'd been imagining what she'd just said.

He froze.

*Josh?* Jode's question echoed like a jolt of lightning into Josh's thoughts.

*Take her?* Jode prodded.

Josh struggled to think. Battled for his self-control. But he was losing his fight and he was losing it fast.

*Do it,* he instructed his brother. There would be hell to pay if they'd heard her wrong.

Cammie shuddered and gasped for air as Josh broke the kiss. She couldn't believe what she'd just said.

*Take me.*

In the beginning of her career this had happened on a couple of occasions. She'd been swept into her arousal and had dated a couple of the male models she'd been in lust with. But upon gaining experience and realizing it was just lust she'd opted to remain professional, giving in only on rare occasions.

Now it was as if she were right back into her past. All the restraint she'd learned over the years was gone and all she wanted was for them to take her. She'd deal with the emotional fallout later. Right now, she just wanted to feel the lust racing through her veins like a wildfire.

Josh's hands were on her breasts again. But this time it was different. He massaged her nipples with strong pulls and tweaks that had her writhing against him. The sound of water splashing was followed by lukewarm droplets falling upon her right shoulder and down her arm. Jode was standing now. She should open her eyes, but she couldn't. Her lids were way too heavy.

"Just go with it," Josh whispered.

*Huh? Go with what?* Her mind was sensually fuzzy as Josh continued seducing her nipples.

"Open your mouth and let Jode in. No worries, we're both clean."

*Oh?* Surprise whispered through her but it was quickly doused by the firmness of his command.

The photo shoot was changing. Shifting quickly into highly sexual energy. Something hot and velvety-hard strained against her mouth. Jode's cock. She parted her lips and he slipped his cockhead inside.

A pinch snapped on her left nipple. A clamp. Vibrations teased her taut nipple. A similar pinch and pulsations snapped through her other nipple. The pressure was exquisite. The cameras continued their whirring.

She moaned as Josh's hands slid around her waist and down her belly. His palms were like two scorching brands. Possessive, hot and firm.

"Lean back against me and widen your thighs so I can get at you better," Josh instructed.

Just thinking of what was happening made her sweetly heady. She pressed herself against him and her back melted into his chest muscles. He groaned as her ass pushed against his tremendous erection. He gyrated his shaft against her ass, pressing forcefully. His palm splayed over her lower abdomen and a hand slipped between her thighs. Need flared quickly. She jerked as a finger slipped between her swollen pussy folds and she cried out when his finger swept over her swollen achy clit. His firm strokes easily lashed away the last restraints of her self-control.

Trembling beneath the onslaught of sensations, Cammie lifted her hands and wrapped them purposefully around Jode's shaft. She squeezed.

*Fuck, I'm getting close!* Josh's curse splintered into Jode's mind. But Jode paid him no heed. He was lost in his own arousal as Cammie's hands latched around his heavy erection like a band indicating how far he could slip into her mouth.

Cammie's seductive tongue was like a pleasure whip as she slurped and sucked like an expert. Looking down at her—his cock in her mouth—rocked his world. The sight was erotic. Her red lips wrapped snugly around his flesh as he sunk in and out had him perched right at the edge of his restraint. He was seconds away from coming.

Every one of her whimpers tore through him like a seductive tornado. His body and balls had never been tighter. The muscles in his thighs quivered and wicked sensations crawled all over him. Oh man, she was so good.

Despite his overwhelming need for release, Josh fought to focus on pleasuring Cammie. He wanted this first time to be spectacular. Something she would remember always.

Her pussy was warm and creamy as he slipped a couple of fingers inside. He groaned and fought for breath as her muscles greedily clenched around him. She was perfectly tight. He could barely restrain himself from lifting her out of the tub, laying her on her bed and sinking his penis deep into her pussy. But that would have to wait. Right now, Jode was about to come and he would be close behind.

Cammie shuddered against him, her body tensing, her whimpers increasing. When she began gyrating her hips uncontrollably, the friction he need to come made him lose all control.

He exploded.

The combination of the pressure of her clamped nipples, Josh stroking her clit and then plunging his fingers into her vagina and having Jode's cock sliding in and out of her mouth in a wicked rhythm was more than Cammie could handle. As her pussy clenched, she pressed the balls of her feet against the side of the bathtub and pushed her ass hard against Josh's shaft.

Her hands and mouth tightened on Jode's erection. Both men cried out at the same time as they orgasmed. Their shouts snapped through her like firecrackers, pummeling every inch of her with fiery shivers. Each stroke of Josh's fingers into her vagina drove more shudders into her. Every thrust of Jode's cock into her mouth made her whimper and wonder how it could be that two virtual strangers could give her such exquisite pleasure.

Her vision went hazy and she flew into the orgasm as if she had wings. She danced on the stars that burst behind her eyes. Surrendered to the whirlwind of arousal and became so blissfully lost, she didn't care about anything except living inside the incredible pleasure.

It was hypnotizing, and she wanted it to last forever, but slowly the spasms ebbed and the harsh sounds of their heavy breathing raced through the air. Jode withdrew and stepped out of the tub. He grabbed his robe and put it on. He didn't look at her. He seemed...shy.

"Are you okay?" Josh asked softly into her ear. His lips brushed along her earlobe making her shiver.

"Y...yes," she managed to mumble.

Lying against him, his taut and powerful thigh muscles cradling her as they pressed against her hips, made her breaths back up. She hadn't anticipated how easily she would slip out of reality. What had happened was simply unbelievable.

And the safe way she was feeling as she lay here was something she'd been craving for most of her adult life. Until this minute, she hadn't realized how lonely she'd been without a man—or make that two men—in her life.

"I think the pictures will be fantastic, just like what we've experienced. Right, Jode?" Josh said.

Jode nodded and he looked over at them. His lust-filled gaze made contact with hers and a sizzle of wanting him again snapped through her.

Oh heavens, what have they done to her that she wanted more from them?

Josh continued brushing his lips against her sensitive earlobe as if they were two old lovers. She shivered as arousal began whispering through her again.

"I think we should check those pictures and then get straight into the next shoot. Are we in agreement?" Josh asked.

Cammie blinked as both disappointment and relief brushed over her. She wasn't sure what to say or how to react. Should she say "please guys, fuck me some more" or should she just pretend this hadn't happened, as they appeared to be doing?

*Okay, girl, suck it up. Follow their lead. Don't let your emotions get involved.*

No-strings sex might just be the thing she needed to snap her back to the real world. Her reality being career first and relationships last. But that idea just didn't seem to be so important to her anymore.

• • ⟊ • •

*SAY SOMETHING TO HER,* Josh urged Jode as the three of them sat at the kitchen table and silently studied the pictures of the shoot they'd just done. He swore he could see the steam wafting off the laptop, the photos were so erotic.

*No, you say something,* Jode replied.

Josh could feel the sexual tension zipping into his bloodstream as Jode stared at the next photo. The one of the three of them in the tub with Jode's cock in her mouth, Josh kissing Cammie and the dolphin-heart clamps on her lush nipples.

*Apologize for losing control. That's the least we should do,* Jode prodded.

*No, you tell her.*

Dammit, he didn't even know how to start to apologize. He'd never had a tongue-tied problem with a woman before.

*Neither have I,* Jode huffed. His frustration lanced through Josh and it pissed him off.

*We have nothing to apologize for. She wanted to be taken, right?* Josh reminded him.

Jode inhaled and Josh sensed his brother's increasing arousal.

Man, his brother's emotions were like a yo-yo, aroused one minute and frustrated the next.

*She smells so good.*

Josh rolled his eyes and cursed Jode in his mind. If Jode kept going the way he was going they would never meet this damned deadline. And they very well might have screwed up a possible relationship with Cammie too.

•• ⤳ ••

CAMMIE TRIED TO ACT as professional as possible for the rest of the day as they continued shooting more products. But she ached to have the closeness she'd experienced in the tub with the two men. Perhaps it was just lust she was experiencing?

The tender way they'd touched her and spoken to her while they'd had sex couldn't be faked, could it? Was she misreading the caring heat in their gazes as they smiled at her and instructed her into different positions with the other toys?

It was as if a wall had suddenly been erected between her and them. They were acting as if they were afraid of her. Something was wrong, and she needed to know what.

But as the day drew to a close, she hadn't been able to bring up the subject. They had remained professional and wary, and she in turn was unsatisfied with how things were left between them.

Even now, an hour after they'd gone, she was still fussing over why she hadn't broached the subject with them.

The shrill ring of her cell phone busted her from her brooding thoughts and she was glad to see her agent's number flash on the screen.

"Alison, where have you been? I have been trying to get a hold of you," Cammie snapped. Her anger just seemed to tumble out of her and she wished she'd been a bit more diplomatic. She'd just sounded like a spoiled child.

"Sorry, sweets, but I had a family emergency and I had to drop everything. I've just had the first chance to check my messages."

Embarrassment and concern gripped Cammie. She'd been so self-absorbed in her own world she hadn't even thought that Alison might not be returning her calls because she was having a problem.

"Is everything all right? What happened? Is there anything I can do to help?"

"My grandfather had a mild heart attack yesterday. My grandmother is so upset—I just couldn't leave her alone while he was in the hospital. I'm waiting for Mom and Dad to fly in from Florida so they can be with her and my grandfather. But no, there's nothing you can do—but you are sweet to offer."

"I am so sorry. I know you all are so close. I hope he gets better quickly." Sadness made Cammie think about her own family and how she hadn't been in touch with her sisters, her parents and grandparents as much as she should be.

"Me too, sweetie. Me too. So what's up? You mentioned on your messages that you haven't met with the owners of Sexy Toys. I got in touch with them just moments ago and they brought me up to speed. They said they had to leave town on an unexpected business trip. They told me not to worry and you are in very good hands with their replacements. So tell me? Who are these men? Are they cute?"

Cute was an understatement.

"Oh they're doable." Cammie smiled. *Most definitely.*

"Doable? Doable? What does that mean?" Curiosity etched her voice.

"They're cute. They're models, actually. And it is just the three of us doing the shoot."

Silence followed.

"Models? Just the three of you?" She sounded just as doubtful as Cammie had when Josh and Jode had first turned up yesterday and told her the same thing. Gosh, had it only been yesterday?

"One of them is a professional photographer. The shots are excellent. They are going to be a smashing addition to my portfolio."

Should she mention to Alison that the models were identical twins? And that the three of them had had sex? No, she couldn't do that. Alison was in the middle of a family emergency. She needed to get back to her grandparents.

"I better let you go. I'll call you later on in the week and tell you how it went."

"Trying to change the subject. Interesting." Alison laughed. But it wasn't a genuine laugh because Cammie detected the underlying tension.

"Please give your grandparents my best. And if you need to talk or need anything, just ring me up, okay? I'm here for you."

"Thanks—you are a doll. I'd better go. I hear Grandma calling. Take care, sweetie."

"I will. Thanks for calling."

"Bye. Gotta go."

Alison hung up and Cammie bit her bottom lip as tears welled up. What would she do if something happened to her grandparents or other family members? She knew bad things happened to people every day. And that you just never knew if you would see a loved one again when you left them and lived far away.

Maybe she had been pursing her career too much? Maybe she should go back home for a visit? She'd been working so hard and collecting material things, like this house and the garage with a loft she now wanted to build. But would it all bring her happiness if she didn't have anyone to share it with her?

Cammie wiped away her tears and vowed to start thinking more seriously about relationships. Maybe even one with Josh and Jode.

• • ◦✂◦ • •

"DO YOU THINK CAMMIE'S agent bought the story?" Josh asked as he and Jode sat cross-legged on Josh's motel bed and dug into the burgers and fries that room service had sent up.

"How could she not? Unless Earl somehow gets ahold of her and tells her. So far it sounds like Alison has no idea it's the two of us who are the male models. Which reminds me, I talked to Kim, and she says she hasn't seen hide nor hair of Earl around the office since we left town."

"He's probably up to something. I hope he's not going to bother Cammie."

"I'll kill him if he does. But remember how difficult it was for us to get Cammie's address out of her even after we showed her the contracts for the deal?"

"She's very protective of Cammie, so I am confident she won't give him her address. Which reminds me about today..."

"Don't bring up the sex adventure in the bathtub. I won't apologize to her for something that was so beautiful," Josh warned.

"What I wanted to say is that I think we shouldn't have pulled back from her the way we did. I think we upset her. I'm not even sure we're on for the run tomorrow morning. It wasn't mentioned after..."

*It's still on.* Josh said as he took a huge bite out of his burger and groaned at the spicy juices exploding on his tastebuds. *We're not letting her down tomorrow. I can promise you that.*

*Good. I was hoping you'd say that.*

# Chapter Six

CAMMIE WAS DOING HER warm-up stretches in her driveway when Josh and Jode drove up in their van. Truth be told she hadn't been sure they would come for the run, especially after the cold-shoulder attitude they'd given to her yesterday. She wished she had the guts to broach the subject right now, but when they stepped out of their vehicle and threw her some very sexy dimpled grins, her anger and curiosity vanished.

Both men wore loose dark-blue shorts and black muscle T-shirts. Their running shoes were a top brand name and she'd heard from fellow runners those shoes were top of the line for comfort and price. They truly did take their runs seriously.

"Hey, beautiful," Josh called out as he strolled toward her. He stretched his arms over his head, and muscles bunched and bulged in his arms.

*Wow.* Those arms had been wrapped around her just yesterday while they'd lain in the bathtub. While he'd made her orgasm.

Her cheeks grew hot and she concentrated on stretching.

"How are you doing? Sleep well last night?" Jode asked as he began stretching beside the van.

Perhaps she should tell them that she'd masturbated again last night while fantasizing about their bubble bath sex? How would they react if she boldly just said it out loud?

"Like a rock," she admitted. Like a rock, after she'd played with a couple more toys and fallen into an exhausted sleep from her several orgasms.

"Good, good. We've got a long day ahead and Jode and I came up with some very sultry scenes for the rest of the toys," Josh said.

He winked at her and she grew warm, despite the cool foggy morning.

Oh boy, it looked as if it was going to be a sexually tense day, at least on her part. During several more minutes of doing their warm-ups, she explained to them the route she normally took around the lake.

"Seven miles," she said. To her surprise they didn't even flinch.

"Let's get a move on. Daylight is burning," Jode called out as he started running at a slow pace down her driveway.

Josh and she looked at each other and grinned. In a moment, they caught up with him. Cammie stayed in the middle while the men flanked her.

Pride pumped through her as onlookers did a double take watching her running with two men. Actually, she'd always taken her runs alone. She'd preferred it that way. But having Jode and Josh along just seemed natural. They didn't speak, and the three of them quickly got into an easy rhythm.

The run went too quickly for Cammie's liking, and before she knew it they were approaching the bed-and-breakfast bakery. After motioning to them she wanted to detour off the road, they followed.

"Awesome," Jode said quietly as they stepped into the bakery. It smelled of fresh-baked bread and brewing coffee.

"Is this where you got your goodies for yesterday's breakfast?" Josh asked as he sidled beside her in front of the counter where Joyce, the thirty-year-old owner, stood smiling at them from ear to ear. Joyce had always bugged Cammie that she should date, but Cammie had always skirted around the issue.

She nodded and gave Joyce the list of what she'd like to purchase.

"Do you boys want anything?" Cammie asked when Joyce turned away and collected the baked goods and fruit.

They shook their heads. "You about covered everything."

Moments later, when Joyce handed Cammie a Tupperware container filled with her order, Joyce nodded to the men.

"Are you fellows new in town?"

"They're co-workers, actually," Cammie said quickly. "Jode and Josh Midnight, I'd like you to meet Joyce White. She owns and runs this bed-and-breakfast."

Joyce smiled warmly. She extended her hand over the counter and turns shaking hands with both men.

"Tight grips. Nice." Joyce batted her long black eyelashes at them. *What was that supposed to mean?*

"Thanks, ma'am." Jode chuckled. "We do need to keep in shape in our line of work."

"I'll bet," Joyce said. She licked her lips in such a sensual way it made annoyance zip through Cammie. She'd never seen Joyce stare at men so intensely with interest before. As if she wanted to pounce on both of them and add them to her bakery collection of yummies on her shelves.

"Thanks for the food. We're going to enjoy it when we get back to my place," Cammie said. She hoped the jab that they were coming home with her would set Joyce in her place, which was nowhere near her men.

*Her men?*

Oh boy, she must be going nuts to consider Jode and Josh as belonging to her already. She needed to set her head straight on these crazy thoughts. And fast!

*I think Cammie is jealous.* Jode chuckled into Josh's mind. *Look at the way her eyes are sparking with anger.*

*She's got every right to be jealous. That woman wants to get her hooks into us*, Josh warned Jode.

*My radar is up, bro. No worries in that department. I only have eyes for Cammie.*

Josh smiled as they waved goodbye to Joyce and walked outside. He noted the tense way Cammie held herself as they broke into a run. It felt absolutely normal having Cammie running with them. As if she'd been with them always. Too bad she wasn't feeling it yet.

*She will. She will,* Jode answered.

"She seems like a nice lady," Josh said as he grabbed the container from Cammie's clenched hand.

Cammie threw him a tight smile. She said nothing as she released her grip and focused her attention far ahead of the road in front of them, pretending nothing had just happened.

"She's not our type at all, is she, Jode?"

"Not at all," Jode called back.

Cammie's taut smile relaxed and Josh noted her shoulders sagging just a bit in relief.

*Yep, she is definitely jealous. I wonder, is that a good sign, brother?* Josh asked.

*I would think so. It means she's interested in us, but not yet confident that we are fully hers.*

Josh nodded. *It looks as if we will have to rectify that situation, and fast.*

*I hear you, my man. I hear you loud and clear. I think by the end of this day, we will have put any doubts about our interests in her right out of her mind.*

*Agreed!* Jode answered and he winked over Cammie's head at Josh.

• • ᘯ • •

CAMMIE HAD JUST SLIPPED into her bathrobe when a sharp rap erupted at her bedroom door.

"We're not ready, yet, Cammie." It was Jode. He didn't open the door but continued to speak on the other side.

"We've decided to take the shoot down to the main-floor bathroom. It has a shower stall and it's perfect for what we have planned."

"Okay, I'll join you in a few minutes." She tried to keep her voice light and airy, as if she didn't have a care in the world. As if she was the utmost professional. But she was feeling anything but confident as she listened to his footsteps fade away.

Cammie wanted to run down to that bakery and pluck out Joyce's false eyelashes and shove them down her throat. How dare she bat her eyelashes at Jode and Josh? She didn't even know them.

And why had Jode and Josh acted perfectly normal over breakfast? Acting as if that woman hadn't been drooling over them? Aside from that one comment from Josh about her not being their type, they hadn't mentioned her again.

While the two men had been busy taking turns taking showers in the main floor bathroom, she'd angrily prepared the table for breakfast. Then she'd gone for her shower and afterward, found them in the kitchen. They had changed into fresh clothing and were eating like wolves, just like yesterday morning. Their eyes had spoken of lust and interest while they'd chatted about what a lovely run they'd had and wouldn't it be fun to get together ever morning and run around the lake?

*Yeah, right. Who are they fooling? Once the deadline is met, they are gone.* A spring of tears bit against the back of her eyes at the thought of her probably never seeing them again.

Oh crap, she was already hopelessly in lust with them. Especially after what had gone down in the bathroom yesterday.

*No-strings sex.* She'd been able to convince herself of that yesterday but today she wasn't so sure. She wanted more than just sex from them. Dammit, she wanted a relationship with both of them. She knew she was thinking like a naïve teenager. Knew reality was nothing like fantasy. Relationships required lots of work and love, and that was with one man. Here she was wanting two of them after just a quick fuck while sitting in a bathtub full of freaking bubbles.

Gosh, was she desperate or what? Cammie frowned and glanced at the full-length mirror hanging on her bedroom door. The older woman staring back at her was just that. Distressed and older than those two younger men.

Sure, she was still fit due to her taking good care of herself, but she had at least ten years on them. She shook her head and bit her bottom lip. She'd been silly in thinking anything permanent would happen between her and Jode and Josh.

*Silly. Silly. Silly.*

•  •  ⚘  •  •

"IT'S CALLED THE ON the Go, Go Girl Vibe, for career women who travel for business and want their pleasure when they are on the go," Jode explained as, minutes later, Cammie stood in the main floor bathroom.

It was toasty in here, despite the lone bathroom window being wide open and the bathroom fan buzzing at top speed. Water streamed out of the showerhead. Red, lit candles were placed on the nearby corner shelf, flickering and giving a romantic appearance—but that wasn't what held her full attention. She stared at the large red vibrator stuck to the shower stall wall via dual immense suction cups. The vibrator was set at her pussy height beneath the showerhead, the vibe shaft angling upward much as an erection would, and it was just as big as Josh and Jode's cocks.

She trembled as she imagined what the men expected her to do with that vibe while they watched.

Farther up the wall, above the vibrator and around breast height and set as far apart as her two nipples, were two life-sized red vinyl mouths with partially opened lips. Their bases were suction-cupped to the wall.

"Picture this. Close-ups with the shower running. Droplets caressing your flushed skin. The vibe sinking into your pussy. Your nipples being massaged by two mouths," Josh said and continued. "Despite its length, the vibe is compact, totally waterproof and fully washable. It folds at the base just above the scrotum and halfway up the shaft. It's virtually seamless, so you won't feel the grooves of the folds while it is in erect position. There's a powerful engine in the scrotum and the rechargeable solar batteries are in the shaft. The vibe is guaranteed to give a woman a fantastic orgasm and it fits perfectly in luggage for the girl on the go." Josh paused for a moment. She suspected it was so she could absorb the picture he was painting.

"As for the two mouths, we call them Ménage Mouths, and they come with the vibe in a kit. They attach to the wall via powerful state-of-the-art suction cups. The lips tremble and suck just like real mouths and also run on rechargeable batteries. A base for all accessories is included in the kit. We'll get close-up shots while you are using the toys. Then later, Jode will stand behind you and his cock will enter your ass. This will show the girl on the go that she can be double-penetrated using her handy solar-powered vibe along with her man of the evening while imagining men's or ladies' mouths sucking her nipples. There is also a third mouth that can be installed on the wall for her to kiss but we left that out of this shoot because I want you facing the camera."

*Oh my gosh.* Her senses sparkled with awareness. Amazing ideas. She would have to get herself one of those kits.

"Go ahead," Josh ordered. "I've got the cameras and video receiving views at different angles. All you have to do is ride the vibe and let the mouths make love to your breasts. I'll take the shots, zooming outward as you go, and then Jode will join you."

She blew out a tense breath and beside her Jode stiffened.

Ride the vibe. Mouths at her breasts? And then Jode fucking her ass? She grew heady. During previous shoots over the years she'd been anally penetrated, so it wasn't new to her. But to have Jode—a man she was attracted to—to be doing her was simply arousing.

"Make the masturbation as real as you want—don't hold back. Just enjoy yourself. We want sultry, sexy and oh-how-I-love-my-vibe look. When Jode joins you he'll be wearing a condom and heavily lubed, so we won't anticipate too much of a problem of him entering you."

Josh made it sound so matter-of-fact. Like it was just business. That's how she used to think of it too until she'd met these two guys. How in the world had she gotten her emotions tangled into this situation? And why didn't she want to get herself out of it?

No strings, she reminded herself as she removed her robe and hung it on a hook. Behind her both men inhaled sharply. She could feel the heat of their gazes as they looked upon her nakedness while she walked past them and the cameras positioned on tripods. Inwardly, she smiled. She was having an effect on them.

Cammie's heart hammered as she neared the lifelike vibrator and the mouths. She studied the engorged clit stimulator, the attached scrotum and the long shaft, which was interwoven with a raised web of veins. The shaft looked to be about eight inches long, with a two-inch girth.

"The vibe comes in various lengths and widths," Jode explained.

She couldn't hear the slurp of lube above the pounding water from the showerhead, but from the corner of her eye she caught site of Jode massaging some ointment onto his condomed shaft.

She wet her lips as nervous tension whispered through her. Then she stepped into the stall. The water was perfect as it cascaded against her collarbone and down her belly and legs. Positioning herself in the stall, she angled her hips nearer to the big vibrator, trying hard not to get so close as to touch it. If she did, she just might start riding it before Josh was ready with the cameras.

Her body hummed with awareness as the water pummeled her flesh and she took a moment to study the sculpted contours of Jode's chest muscles before angling her gaze over his flat belly to his thickening erection as he applied the lube. Her gaze rose and met his. His eyes were dark with intention as he observed her.

"Okay, Cammie, go ahead," Josh urged in a tight voice. "The on switch is at the bottom of the scrotum. The mouths are already activated. All you need to do is touch them and they'll initiate action."

She reached beneath the scrotum, found the small switch and flipped it. The vibe was warm and flesh-like to her touch and it made a low purring sound as it trembled to life. Not daring to glance at Jode or Josh again, she stepped closer to the vibrator.

"Closer, Cammie," Josh urged softly. "Ride it."

Her thighs tightened and she shuddered at his seductive voice. Angling her lower body nearer to the wall, she inhaled as the plum-shaped cockhead pushed past her pussy lips and slid deep into her vagina. The pressure was intense and her muscles eagerly gripped the powerful intruder.

The cameras whirred and clicked. She wished herself to move into the "zone" that she enjoyed so much, but it didn't happen. All she wanted was for Jode and Josh to step into the shower and fuck her.

Urgency rippled through her and she moved her upper body until her rigid nipples were inserted into the two red mouths. Instantly the mouths clamped snugly around her taut flesh. She stilled as the warm lips began to pull and knead. Electrified pleasure mingled with sweet pain as it zipped through her buds. The sensations arrowed down her belly into her pussy. Instinctively she arched, pushing her tender nipples deeper into the sucking mouths.

She surged against the wall. Her clit met the stimulator and it began trembling and massaging her incredibly sensitive flesh. The shaft grew warmer and throbbed inside her pussy.

"Gyrate your hips, Cammie," Josh instructed.

She did as he asked and moaned softly as exquisite sensations rippled through her. She fought to remain in control.

Oh man. This was going to kill her. The heat of arousal swept deeper. She closed her eyes tightly and slipped into the pleasure stream, not caring anymore if they were watching.

"Imagine that vibe being a man in the shower with you," Josh said in an indulgent voice. "Who would he be, Cammie? Can you imagine him?"

She nodded, picturing Josh in front of her, his cock plunging inside her.

"Now imagine two other men sucking at your nipples," Jode said from immediately behind her.

She tensed. Jode had stepped into the shower with her.

"Don't stop, Cammie," Josh said. "You're doing great. Open your eyes and gaze dreamily into the camera. I'm loving that sultry look on your face."

She found it incredibly hard to open her eyes but she managed.

Her breaths quickened as Josh stood there beside his tripods and lights, the cameras clicking away. He must have put his gear on timers as he was watching Jode and her in the shower stall. He lifted his top over his head and a whimper escaped her lips as dominant muscles swelled in his arms. She raised her gaze and identified lust shining brightly in his eyes.

"Jode is going to lube you, Cammie. It'll make things easier for you."

She nodded, and writhed against the vibe and ménage lips. Heat from Jode's body splayed against her back and his hand slipped around her waist, his palm branding her lower belly as he held her in position. A heavily lubed finger prodded at her sphincter and she inhaled sharply.

"Easy, just breathe and stay as relaxed as you can," Jode whispered.

She nodded and moaned as his finger entered her ass. Her legs grew weak. His finger pulled out. A moment later, it slipped into her again with another load of lube. He probed her ass gently, pushing the lube against her quivering anal muscles.

"That's it, Cammie. Let Jode do what needs doing."

She trembled.

Josh's expression was tight and aroused as he unzipped his pants.

*Oh my gosh.*

He pulled down his jeans and stepped out of them. His erection—a massive, bulging knot of flesh—was perfectly outlined against his underwear.

"That's it, Cammie, play to the cameras. You're beautiful." Josh's voice was dark and thick.

Playing? Who was playing?

She shivered as he slipped his hand beneath the waistband of his underwear and brought out his shaft. It was long and swollen, flushed red with arousal.

"She's ready," Jode growled.

Josh nodded once. His eyes darkened with fire. Heat throbbed through her as the water cascaded against her sensitive skin.

Jode removed his fingers from her ass and she gasped at the firm pressure of his lubed cockhead pushing past the tight bundle of muscles. She inhaled a tormented breath and arched against him, her anus eagerly clenching his impalement. Closing her eyes, she embraced the pressure his cock created as it slid deep into her.

*Fuck! She's so damned tight. Perfectly tight,* Jode moaned to his brother as Cammie's strong anal muscles gripped his shaft.

*I can feel her,* Josh answered. *So tight around my cock.*

Jode smiled and kissed Cammie's warm neck. He removed his palm from her abdomen and smoothed his hands over her hips, holding her tight. He bucked against her. She whimpered and held still for him, allowing him to thrust slowly in and out of her ass. He knew the rhythm would give her a deeper impalement of both his shaft and the vibe, creating a greater friction against her clit.

*I think we should tell her how much we want her,* Jode whispered. There was a passionate need to tell her the truth, at least the truth about how they craved her so badly. That they wanted to take her to bed and make love to her over and over again. And they wanted to do it now.

*She needs to know,* Josh agreed. *We need to show her.*

Josh was impressed. Cammie was an expert in the way she posed so naturally for the cameras, so despite Jode fucking her sweet ass and regardless of the arousal that must be coursing through her, she was composed. Any lesser model would pretend she was masturbating, but Cammie had let herself loose and it showed.

Her lips were parted as she panted and her eyes were heavy-lidded as she struggled to look at the camera.

He could tell that she wanted to come. Bad.

Josh had gasped as the vibrator sunk into Cammie's vagina, fantasizing it was him thrusting into her. He'd enjoyed the frantic way her hips moved in a sensual dance, gyrating as if she were doing a striptease while impaled on the vibe, her nipples captured by the Ménage Mouths. Her sexy whimpers as Jode pierced her behind nearly made him lose control and he'd almost dropped to his knees as her tight anal muscles clamped around his brother's shaft.

Now it was his turn to penetrate her. To claim her.

The time was right to make love to her and to show her they wanted much more than just sex from her.

Cammie shuddered at Jode's possessive thrusts and moaned at the sultry way Josh stalked toward her. Instinctively she knew this wasn't for show but for real.

"The cameras are off. This is our time now," Josh said.

He held out his hand to her. Wild hunger rose within Cammie as she placed her palm in his. Jode stopped thrusting and allowed her to move off the vibrator and away from the intriguing Ménage Mouths.

The men quickly angled her so that Jode's back was against the shower stall wall and she was in front of him. His hands slid possessively around her waist and his cock once again slipped into her ass. Water pummeled her breasts but it stopped when Josh stepped in front of her and took the brunt of the splashes.

"We instantly knew you were the woman for us," he said as he gripped her other hand and intertwined their fingers. His eyes blazed with passion. A sweet smile curled the sides of his mouth.

"We both felt an intensely rich reaction when we saw your pictures in that conference room. We've never been this wildly attracted to the same woman before. A woman we barely know. The attraction is so powerful, so penetrating, so full of desire for you. There are things we need to confess, but not now. Right now, we need to make love to you. To show you that you will always be the only woman for us. We need you to know how much we want you and how much more we want from you."

Cammie's thoughts whirled. Was she hearing him right? Or had she slipped into a wicked and wonderful fantasy? She ached to be loved. To be held by both of them. It was crazy. It was reality.

Josh's expression was sincere. She could tell by the firm set of his jaw, the erotic way their fingers intertwined and the incredibly tender way Jode's hands held her hips that he spoke from his heart.

But it didn't make sense. How could they have such strong feelings for her from some photos on a wall? What else did they need to tell her?

"I want to kiss you," Josh whispered. "I've been dying to taste your lips again. And know that when I kiss you, Jode feels it too. When he fucks your ass, I feel it and it is sensational."

Her thoughts swirled and her eyes widened with surprise. They had that kind of a bond?

His eyes closed and the expression on his face turned savage with need. His head lowered and his mouth covered hers. All her thoughts and doubts disintegrated as his lips devoured hers.

Beautiful shock waves cascaded through her. Her body jerked against Jode and she cried into Josh's mouth as his condomed erection plunged into her in one swift thrust. His cock was hard and ultra-thick as he entered her vagina. Harder and heavier than any other man that she'd had sex with. He impaled her so deeply and so thoroughly it was as if her entire being was being claimed.

They didn't allow her to catch her breath or her thoughts. Within seconds, the twins found a fascinating rhythm that shattered her senses. Electric shudders exploded through her like an unleashed storm and she was cast into a pleasure world she'd never experienced before. Colors ricocheted behind her closed eyes and exquisite sensations raged through her. She moaned as her pussy and anal muscles contracted simultaneously around Josh and Jode's shafts. Both men groaned their appreciation and pumped harder into her.

Josh's kisses became hotter and more intense. Jode's lips melted against her neck. Each thrust drove her pleasure higher until it twirled around her like a searing tornado. It embraced her. Scorched her. Loved her. Possessed her.

She was theirs and they were hers.

This was crazy. But crazy good.

• • ❧ • •

"NOT BAD, EH?" JODE chuckled from his perch on a kitchen chair as the three of them studied the photos from the shower shoot on the laptop.

After they'd double-penetrated her, taking her to such intriguing pleasure heights, they'd showered with her in the stall. After they'd finished, they'd wrapped her snugly in her robe and donned theirs as well.

The loving and caring way Jode had led her down the stairs with her pussy and ass aching so wonderfully made Cammie realize these men were not toying with her. He'd led her into the kitchen where he'd found ingredients to make omelettes, and her heart was still pitter-pattering with disbelief at how lucky she'd become.

He'd cooked for her, informing her that she'd better get used to a lot of kitchen time as both he and Josh loved to cook and eat after they made love. She'd not dared to ask him how many other women they'd had sex with because suddenly it just didn't matter. Joyce and her false eyelashes be damned. Jode and Josh belonged to Cammie and she sensed they would never stray.

Shortly after, when the omelets were ready in the skillet, Josh had shown with his laptop loaded with the new photos and video.

"Not bad is an understatement, bro. When customers get a look at these photos it will singe their false eyelashes," Josh replied.

Cammie hid a giggle, wondering if they had realized Joyce's eyelashes were indeed false or if his words were just a coincidence.

The photos of Jode and herself leapt off the laptop screen. Water beads glistened on their skin and the candles added the romantic touch.

"You're an excellent photographer," she admitted.

Josh gazed up at her. He looked absolutely serious when he said, "Without you, we would be nothing."

Her cheeks grew warm as Jode chimed in, "You are the most beautiful woman in the world."

She laughed and shook her head. These guys were absolutely sweet.

"You won't be saying that when I'm full of wrinkles and white hair and you're still in your prime."

Jode shook his head. "We'll all grow old together, gracefully and embracing it as it comes. As Josh told you earlier, we've never reacted this way before to a woman. Not this intensely. Both of us. Together. We know deep in our guts that you are the one for us."

"I've been meaning to ask you about that. Exactly how does this bond work?"

Jode suddenly stood and began gathering the plates from the table while Josh began to explain.

"Up until puberty we were like a lot of other twins. We could hear what the other was thinking, we finished each other's sentences, one of us was outgoing—meaning me—and the other was a bit more reserved, meaning Jode."

"And then puberty hit," Jode explained as he placed the dishes into the sink.

"Suddenly, we began to like the same girls," Josh continued. "We learned not to finish each other's sentences, as it seemed to irk them. We tried to not like the same girl, but it was hell when one of us was out on a date and the other could literally feel what was going on sexually."

"It was embarrassing at the beginning," Jode replied as he returned and sat back down.

"To say the least." Josh laughed, and Cammie inhaled as that sexy dimple popped out in his cheek. "I mean, puberty is a bitch without the additional complications of feeling your twin's sexual excitement. As we grew older, we seriously kept trying not to fall for the same girl, but our bodies and minds persisted and we continued to do so."

Jode went on. "But the girls in question caught on quickly that both of us were sexually attracted to them. Most didn't want to have anything to do with twins in their bed."

"And quite frankly, we weren't into the idea either. We had come to the conclusion that we were either going to grow old alone or wait until the perfect woman came along and accepted both of us."

Jode nodded. "And we have no explanation as to why, but when we saw your photographs..."

"It was as if a light bulb went off in our heads and explosions snapped through our bodies. We just had to meet you and when we did, we noticed immediately that you were attracted to the both of us," Josh finished.

Cammie couldn't stop herself from smiling. Happiness flooded through her. These two were so cute when they continued each other's sentences. So endearing. How could a woman not fall for them?

"But we hardly know each other." She needed for them to see that what they were explaining just didn't make sense. It just wasn't normal for two men to fall for her so quickly.

*Oh crap!* Who was she kidding? Normal was boring. Two men were better than one. Who was she to question their feelings for her when she could see what they spoke was the truth? She did feel an attraction for both of them. She'd be stupid to not follow her instincts where they were concerned, but she still had questions.

"I mean, lots of people are sexually attracted to each other and then it fizzles, and then there's nothing there for them to work on. And here I have two of you," she explained. In that split second all her doubts flooded back.

Josh grinned at her. "It seems we have some more convincing to do, brother."

"Much, much more convincing," Jode agreed.

Both men stood.

Cammie swallowed as they towered over her. To her surprise, they removed their robes and set them on the backs of their kitchen chairs. Her eyes widened at their massive erections.

Good God! Did she turn them on this much?

"We aren't your normal men, Cammie," Jode said as he extended his hand to her.

"And we will prove it to you over and over again, sweetheart, and not just with sex." Josh held out his hand to her as well.

"Much more than just sex," Jode affirmed. "We're romantic and love a woman who is intelligent."

"As you most certainly are." Josh smiled.

Once again her doubts were dashed and she placed her hands in both of theirs. Their strong fingers curled and intertwined with hers.

They pulled her into a standing position in front of them. They towered over her and she felt safe because of their size and protected by this newfound love.

# Chapter Seven

"WHAT? NO TOYS THIS time?" Cammie teased as Josh and Jode finished tying her wrists and ankles to her bedposts. They'd used some of the Sexy Toys straps they'd had in one of their toy boxes and she was surprised that she didn't feel an ounce of fear at allowing them to tie her up. Trust like she experiencing was heavenly.

"Boy toys." Josh's lips tilted into a sexy smile that had her heart racing.

"Well-hung boy toys." Cammie chuckled, but her laugh stopped short as both men dropped their robes.

Sweet mercy! Their erections were...immense. Better than well-hung.

Excitement surged. She began to tremble.

"What have you two planned for me?" she asked as both men climbed onto the bed. Josh moved between her spread legs, his hands warm as he placed them on her thighs. Jode lay on his belly and using his elbows for support, angled his upper body over her chest, his head hovering over her left breast.

"It's a little late to ask what we're up to, don't you think, sweetness?" Jode said.

Cammie breathed roughly as he lashed the tip of her nipple with his moist tongue.

"And even if she had asked, we wouldn't have spoiled the surprise," Josh said gently. His hot breath fanned teasingly against her inner thighs.

"Surprise?" she asked.

"You'll be surprised at what we can do with our mouths, love," Jode said.

Oral. They were doing oral on her. With her being bound! She should have known it would be something naughty. Bastards.

He kissed her nipple tenderly, teasingly with feather-light strokes. Once, twice, three times. She moaned as erotic sensations awakened within her.

Heat breathed against her pussy and she jolted as Josh licked between her labia, swiping his tongue along her engorged clit.

She whimpered as Jode cupped her left breast. While he continued to kiss her nipple, he brushed a shoulder against the tip of her other nipple. The erotic skimming of his flesh against hers had her moaning at the incredible sparks of arousal.

"Ingenious," she whispered to him.

He grinned around her nipple, then opened his mouth and sucked her bud between his hot lips. His mouth tightened and his teeth nibbled, making Cammie inhale sharply at the bursts of pleasure-pain.

Josh caressed and lapped her clit, and within seconds he had her panting and gyrating her hips.

They tended to her that way for a long time, their slurps mingling with her moans. When Jode stopped and moved off her and away from her breasts, she protested, pulling at her restraints. She wanted him back there making love to her nipples with that delightful mouth of his.

Jode stretched out sideways along her left side, his face close to hers. She shivered as he pressed the powerful brand of his hard cock against the outside of her thigh and began to gyrate his hips, pushing his swollen erection along her flesh.

"No worries, darling," he whispered. His eyes were dark with lust and sparkled with unmistakable love as he reached out a hand and cupped her breast. He began a slow, seductive massage of her flesh.

His head lowered. Her breath halted as his mouth melted over hers in a firm kiss that rocked all of her senses. It was an intoxicating kiss and he showed her how deeply he cared about pleasuring her.

*Wow.*

Between her thighs Josh lapped hungrily, his tongue a whip of pleasure. She groaned and pulled at the restraints as his tongue slipped into her vagina and out again to return to firmly massaging her clit.

*Wonderful.*

Soon she was lost inside the pleasure their tongues created. She wasn't a person anymore, but a bundle of need waiting and wanting to explode. But they kept her on the edge as she bucked her hips trying to get release from Josh's tongue and moaned into Jode's succulent mouth as he mated with her tongue.

Cammie loved this. The incredible torture, the slow, deliberate lashes of their tongues that overloaded her senses, and the naughty straps that held her captive to the two men.

When she began begging around Jode's frantic kisses for them to take her, to make love to her, they were quick to respond. They unlashed her bonds and she was free to wrap her arms around Jode's neck as he continued to kiss her, while at the same time he ripped a foil-encased condom and rolled it onto his engorged flesh.

Heat flared as she heard the slurp of lube from somewhere beside the bed and she knew it was Josh preparing his cock.

A moment later, Jode's hands settled firmly on her waist. He lifted her high over him and angled her body onto his torso. She tucked her legs onto each side of his hips, bending her knees so that she was squatting. As he brought her down, she inhaled sharply as his cockhead nudged against her wet vagina. Pressure and pleasure made her gasp. His penispenetrated her in a swift plunge that made her frantically grab his shoulders and kiss him wildly.

Cammie began to gyrate her hips, looking for the pleasure and needing a powerful release. She barely felt Josh's strong hands curl over her shoulders. He dug his fingers into her flesh and gently pushed until her body was fully on top of Jode's. She kept kissing Jode, loving the sparks created in the erotic way their tongues dashed against each other and mated.

Pressure erupted against Cammie's sphincter as Josh stroked his lubed shaft into her ass, slamming in quickly and right to the hilt. She gasped into Jode's mouth at the exquisite tightness of having a dual penetration. It heightened her senses and she loved the pressure of being doubly filled. Josh withdrew and plunged into her again and again.

He kept up a rough, powerful rhythm. The intense movement made Jode's pubic bone rub her clit, which sent trembles of pleasure whipping through her, making her vaginal muscles clench around Jode's cock.

He growled into her mouth and kissed her harder.

Cammie's orgasm exploded, blinding her with sparks. Pleasure embraced her, tangled around her and held her captive. She bucked against Josh, gyrated with Jode.

Josh's strokes became frantic, faster and more powerful. Beneath her, Jode's body tightened, responding to the stimulation created by his brother, and she knew Jode was nearing his climax. His erection throbbed inside her, the heat of it was immense and perfect.

It was good. So good.

With every impalement, Josh's grunts grew louder. He was nearing his release.

Cammie tensed, ripped her mouth from Jode's and cried out as her climax intensified and fully grabbed ahold of her, tossing her into the kaleidoscope of wicked sensations that made love to her entire being. She lost her breath and surrendered to the shudders whipping through her.

So sweet. So beautiful. So perfect.

• • ⚬ • •

JOSH STARED AT THE tender way Jode tucked a sleeping Cammie beneath the abundance of blankets. His heart fluttered at the intimate sight. He knew they had truly found the one woman who would accept them both. They'd known her for three days, and it was as if she had always been in their lives.

"I've never felt so satisfied," Jode whispered as he got up off the bed and walked to stand beside Josh. They both continued to gaze at her. Long black eyelashes framed her closed eyes, pink blushed her cheeks and her sweet, plump red lips were slightly parted.

"I've never felt so accepted," Josh replied.

Cammie was a passionate woman and she hadn't blinked an eye when they'd confessed that both of them wanted to be with her.

Jode nodded. "I know what you mean. And she's so trusting. I just love that about her."

"The perfect fit," Josh said.

"The perfect woman," Jode added.

The forever woman. The only woman for them.

•• ◦∽ ••

CAMMIE DIDN'T KNOW how they managed to meet the deadline because they had sex before, during and after every shoot. The men slept over every night and took her out on romantic dinner dates every evening. Early mornings were set aside for their runs and visits to the bakery. Once Joyce saw how happy Cammie was and how the men ignored her fluttering of her false eyelashes, she began to act normal again.

That Sexy Toys had wanted her based on the photos from twenty years earlier, photos that were still hanging in Sexy Toys' conference room, was still unbelievable to Cammie. Whenever she brought up the subject, the men eased her fears by making love to her or reassuring her that Sexy Toys knew what they were doing.

The tender, caring way they treated her and made love to her had removed every single one of her doubts. They wanted a relationship.

On Friday morning, they insisted she take the day off and remain at home while they went to do the presentations to the owners of Sexy Toys. She'd agreed, not really wanting to see the people who'd let her down when she'd worked there. After promising her they would have a serious talk, as they had a confession to make when they returned by late evening, they'd waved goodbye before she could ask any questions.

Seeing their van disappear down her driveway, loneliness unlike anything she'd ever experienced before swept over Cammie. Jode and Josh weren't even gone two minutes and she'd hurried inside, deciding she would head to Sexy Toys after all. She would simply surprise them.

• • ᴄᴩᴏ • •

THE RECEPTIONIST—WHO admitted she was a temp—hadn't been able to locate the owners or Josh and Jode. She'd told Cammie to head down to the conference room and she would send the first person she could as soon as possible. So Cammie stood in front of the room and was about to knock when the unmistakable gravelly voice of Earl sent icy shivers snaking up her back.

"You bitch." He scowled. He came up behind her faster than a snake. Surprise and fear crashed into her as he grabbed her by her left shoulder and swung her around so quickly she didn't even know what was happening. In an instant, he had her pinned against the door, unable to move, his hot hand covering her mouth.

Panic pushed aside Cammie's shock and she struggled against his iron grip. She couldn't move an inch. She screamed, but all that came out was a screech that wouldn't alert anyone unless they were nearby.

"You made me lose my fucking job," he growled.

His hot, alcohol-drenched breath slammed into her face, making her tummy twist with revulsion.

"I couldn't find you." He slurred his words. "That bitch agent of yours was unreachable and no one would give me your address or phone number. Now you and those bastards came through on the deadline and I got let go."

What was he talking about?

Earl's gray eyes glazed with anger and his face glowed red with rage. He'd aged since she'd last seen him. Aged, and not for the better.

Cammie tried to turn her face away from him so she could inhale some fresh air, but he held his grip on her mouth, forcing her to inhale his rancid stench. His lusty sneer, the liquor fumes and her panic made her lightheaded. Nausea roiled violently in her stomach as her past crashed in around her.

She'd been young and stupid and inexperienced with workplace ethics back then. She should have gone to the cops about Earl, but this was an adult business and she'd feared the authorities would just say she was asking for it. Instead, she'd taken the easy way out and sold her shares of the business to her partner—Earl's drinking buddy—who'd refused to help her where Earl was concerned, and she'd quit Sexy Toys.

Defiance pushed aside Cammie's fear. This time she wouldn't let Earl get away with harassing her. This time she was going to fight back! But how? She struggled to come up with an escape but his next words had her focusing on what he was saying.

"I thought for sure you wouldn't do that modeling gig. You're such an uptight bitch. Figured you wouldn't give into those Midnight brothers. It was hard not to notice they fucked you during those shoots. Pleasure like that can't be faked on a woman's face." His voice was garbled and she could barely hear him.

Damn him! He'd already seen the pictures. Anyone else seeing them would not bother her at all. It was her job. Her profession. But with Earl, she felt horribly dirty and unbelievably vulnerable. It was a feeling she'd never again wanted to experience in her life, but here was Earl whipping the disgust she felt about him and she felt the helplessness for not being able to control the situation she'd been in while working here all those years ago. The suffocating revulsion sliced through her like a sledgehammer. She wanted him off her.

Cammie tried to wrench her arms free from where they were crushed against Earl's chest, but he held her so tightly with his body she couldn't even move her legs in order to step on his toes.

"Yeah, you fucked them and I lost the bet, you little bitch."

Her mouth went dry. *Bet? What bet?*

Earl's glassy eyes widened as if he understood she had no clue as to what he was saying.

"You didn't know about the bet, did you? For them to get you into bed by the deadline or they would lose Sexy Toys to me. Now you know, bitch."

*No!* Her senses reeled.

"Get the fuck off her, you slimy piece of shit!"

Jode! His shout shot a huge slice of relief through Cammie.

In a split second, Jode and Josh appeared. They tore Earl off her and Josh pounded his fist into Earl's face. Blood spurted and Cammie's tummy knotted in despair at the sound of breaking bones. Then Josh punched Earl in the gut. The man screamed, doubling over.

Two security guards appeared out of nowhere and grabbed Earl by his shoulders, forcing him to stand straight. He snarled at her, streams of blood rolling from his nose.

"Enjoy your fucking life, bitch!" he grumbled.

Nausea clutched at Cammie's belly at the anger boiling in Earl's eyes. Instinctively, she knew he truly hated her because she had never given into his sexual advances in order to keep her job.

"We are pressing assault charges. Tell that to the police when you call them," Josh ordered.

The guards nodded and quickly hustled Earl down the hallway.

It was then she noticed Kim hovering nearby. Her old friend had aged over the years and she had the same frightened look that Cammie had once seen in her own eyes before she'd finally quit Sexy Toys.

Kim looked as if she'd been crying. Her eyes were swollen and red.

"I...I told them...about Earl. I'm sorry I...betrayed your confidence," Kim said as tears streaked black rivers of mascaradown her cheeks. Her lips were trembling and her hands shook violently as she dabbed at her eyes with a tissue.

Concern for her old friend had Cammie reaching out and grasping both of Kim's hands. They were ice cold.

"It's all right, Kim. Everything is going to be all right," she said, trying to reassure her. Kim tossed her a wobbly smile.

"I'm glad you came back. I missed you," she said.

"I missed you too, sweetie. I'm so sorry I didn't keep in touch. I was just trying to bury the past. I hope you understand."

Kim nodded jerkily.

"They fired Earl," Kim said quickly. "I should have told them about Earl the day they purchased Sexy Toys...but I was afraid...that they didn't care..." Kim turned to face Josh and Jode. They smiled at her reassuringly.

"But they do care," she sobbed. "They truly do. I...if you'll excuse me, I have to get cleaned up and wash my face. I look awful when I cry. I don't want to scare my kids when I go home."

"Sure, sure. You take care, Kim." Cammie let go of her hands and took comfort that they had already grown warm. Kim was strong. She was going to be okay. Her friend nodded and gave Josh and Jode one quick adoring glance and then walked quickly down the hall.

As Kim left, the full brunt of what had just happened with Earl made Cammie's knees go to jelly. The full weight of what could have happened had Josh, Jode and Kim not come along when they did made her stumble.

The twins quickly grabbed her before she could slump to the ground. Concern whipped over both their faces as they ushered her into the conference room.

"Ah, shit, Cammie, are you all right?" Jode asked.

She could barely walk, her legs were shaking so badly now. Had they not been holding on to her, she would have sunk to the floor. Jode ushered her into a chair and a moment later Josh thrust a glass full of water against her mouth.

"Drink, beautiful lady," Jode said. His voice shook and she didn't know if it was from rage or fear or both.

Both men crouched onto their haunches in front of her as Cammie sipped the water. The cold liquid was heaven as it exploded over her dry tongue. She closed her eyes and gulped, loving the way the water splashed down her parched throat. When she opened her eyes, their pale faces would have frightened her had she not been otherwise occupied at trying to figure out what Earl had been saying.

"I'm so sorry he came back, Cammie. We had him escorted out over an hour ago after we fired him," Josh said.

*After they fired him?* Had what Earl said been the truth?

Her stomach did a sickening somersault.

"You mean he's gone because of the bet," she managed to say.

Her insides went to jelly as both men looked at each other with horrified expressions on their faces. Those looks of guilt could not be denied. Earl had told her the truth.

"You let me believe you were the male models, but you are the owners," she managed to say as the full of their deception hit her like a ton of bricks.

Oh, she'd been horribly naïve and badly betrayed.

"Bet? You know about it?" Josh gasped. A red flush of embarrassment crossed his face. He cursed and turned away from her.

Jode also swore and buried his face in his hands.

"It wasn't supposed to be this way," he muttered.

"If I knew you both better, I'd think that you two were ashamed of yourselves. Maybe because you've been caught?" she taunted, wanting to hurt them and make them feel her pain.

The both shook their heads and then turned their faces to her. Yes, they were mortified, it was clearly written on their faces.

"Sweetheart, you've got it all wrong," Josh insisted.

"I don't think so. Earl told me about a bet and a deadline about getting me into bed. I filled in the rest." Cammie forced brittle coldness into her voice, despite hoping they had a plausible explanation for this damned bet. All that sex and tenderness and those plans for the future they'd murmured into her ears while making love to her the last couple of days and nights. It all couldn't have been just because of a bet. It just couldn't be...faked. Could it?

When Josh slumped dejectedly into a chair beside her, Cammie knew it had been just what Earl said.

Josh frowned and clenched his hands into trembling fists. He was pissed off, but she would give as good as she got if he tried to weasel his way out of this.

"Okay, it started out that way," Josh admitted.

"Asshole!" she shouted before she could stop herself.

"Hear us out, please?" Jode interjected.

"Fine. Just hurry up. You're both wasting my time." Oh boy, she was going to be sick. She had trusted these two men. She had bought the bullshit they told her and swallowed it hook, line and sinker.

"As I said, it started out as a bet," Josh said. "But only because he was handing us his job if we could hire you as the model. When you opened your door and didn't give us a chance to get in a word edgewise, we just let you believe we were the models."

"Actually, we were going to be the models anyway because we couldn't find anyone at such short notice, so technically..." Jode chimed in.

Josh nodded. "We just didn't tell you about the boss part and before we knew it—"

"We were so far in, we didn't want to ruin things by telling you what was going on," Jode finished.

Both men shrugged and frowned at her.

Cammie shook her head. This was such a big mess. She should be hating them. Slapping them. Shouting at the top of her lungs. But she just didn't have the energy, so she would listen to what they had to say and reserve judgment until she was a bit more clearheaded than now.

"Go on," she said stiffly.

"Having sex wasn't a part of the bet. Jode and I are attracted to you. It was like we said, the instant we saw your pictures. That part we told you is true," Jode said.

Josh quickly broke in. "Everything is true, Cammie. We're attracted to you. We care for you. We love you."

Both of them stared at her with desperation in their eyes.

"What about Earl? Why did you fire him, if not because of the bet?"

Josh answered first. "When we arrived this morning Kim asked to speak with us. She said that Earl had been sexually harassing her for years and he'd been doing the same to you when you worked here. She said she didn't want to break your confidence by telling us you admitted to her that Earl had cornered you once in a back room and would have raped you had you not managed to get away from him."

Cammie shuddered as she remembered how close that had been.

"She said you quit that same day after you reported it to your partner and he laughed and told you to suck it up. We fired Earl and were trying to persuade Kim to press charges with the police when we heard him in the hallway just now."

She inhaled deeply, trying to stifle her anger.

"And of course, that makes everything regarding this bet all right?" Cammie asked.

"No, it doesn't," Josh stated firmly. "We never should have made a bet with him. We should have let him go, but unfortunately no one was talking to us about him until we got an inkling from Kim last week. But she didn't spill the beans until this morning."

"Do you know how horrible I felt knowing Earl was shown those pictures from the photo shoot because of a bet?"

Jode and Josh both tensed.

"That's bullshit," Jode said and they both shook their heads. "Earl never saw anything. He couldn't have because everything is still out in the van. Whatever he said, he's just yanking your chain. Don't let him tear us apart, sweetheart."

"I don't know..."

"On the ride over to Sexy Toys, we decided those photos are going to remain private." Josh smiled. "They'll just be for us. We want you all to ourselves. We love you. Have we said that to you today?"

His smile widened. Of course he knew they had told her they loved her early this morning just before they left.

Her anger cracked and began to fall apart.

"Please, sweetheart." Jode grabbed her hand and held tight. "Please let us explain. Please give us another chance. We wanted to tell you everything tonight when we got back home."

*Home.* That one word melted her anger instantly. That they thought of her place as being their home wrapped warmth around her heart despite her being pissed off. And they did say this morning that they had something very important to tell her. This was it. The bet. And they were the bosses who were so eager to meet her.

Cammie understood what had happened. Truly she did, but she couldn't let the two of them off that easy. They'd been dishonest and yes, she would have to accept some of the blame for her blind trust.

"I think you're going to have to work very hard for my forgiveness, gentlemen."

Relief flashed across both their faces.

"Name it," Josh replied quickly.

"We'll do it. Whatever you want, beautiful lady," Jode said.

She couldn't help but smile. This might be lots of fun.

"Do whatever I ask when we get home, and I just might be inclined to think about maybe forgiving you."

In an instant, Josh's eyes brightened and understanding flared across Jode's face as well.

"We're going home with you?" Jode asked with eagerness.

Cammie nodded.

"Yes!" Josh laughed.

"Thankfully, we have that box of toys to play with when we get back, and I love to eat after lovemaking. You'll have to cook and clean for me..."

Josh and Jode laughed, their arms slipping protectively around her waist as they led her to the door. Their powerful touches made her feel safe again, Earl be damned. She knew the statute of limitations of sexual harassment in her case had long passed, but she was going to press assault charges against Earl for what had just happened and she would persuade Kim to go after him for sexual harassment.

And yes, she'd make Josh and Jode work hard for her forgiveness. Very hard indeed and she would love every minute of it too.

**The End**

# Mini Catalog

~ Jan Springer ~ Erotic Romance ~

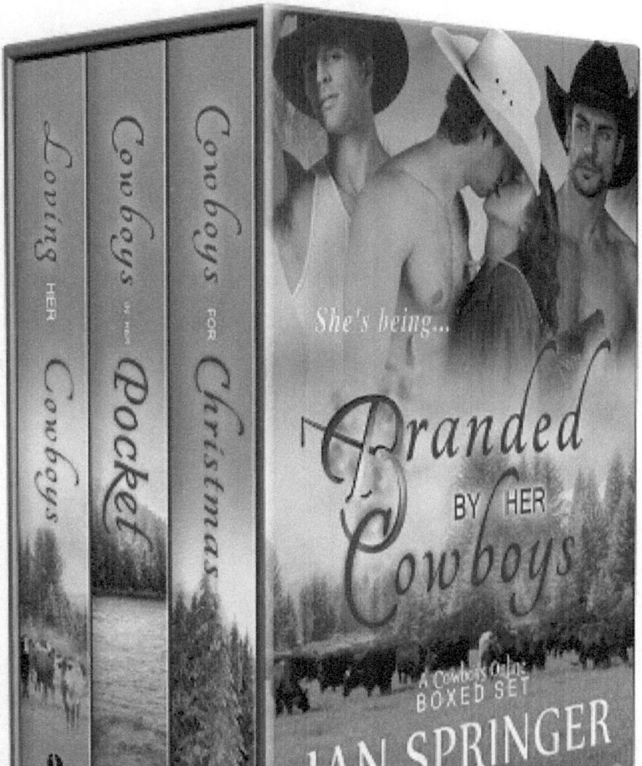

Loving HER Cowboys

Cowboys IN HER Pocket

Cowboys FOR Christmas

She's being...

Branded BY HER Cowboys

A Cowboys OF THE
BOXED SET

JAN SPRINGER

NEW YORK TIMES & USA TODAY
BESTSELLING AUTHOR

3
2
1

Branded by Her Cowboys Boxed Set
Includes the first three books in the Cowboys Online series.
Cowboys for Christmas, Cowboys in her Pocket and Loving Her
Cowboys

JENNIFER JANE (JJ) Watson has spent the past ten Christmases in a maximum-security prison. The last thing she expects is to get early parole, along with a job on a remote Canadian cattle ranch serving Christmas holiday dinners to three of the sexiest cowboys she's ever met!

Rafe, Brady and Dan, thought they were getting a male ex-con to help out around their secluded ranch, but instead they get an attractive and very appealing female. In the snowbound wilds of Northern Ontario, female companionship is rare. It's a good thing the three men like to share.

They're dominating, sexy as sin, and they fill JJ with the hottest ménage fantasies she's ever had. Suddenly she's craving cowboys for Christmas and wishing for something she knows she can never have...a happily ever after.

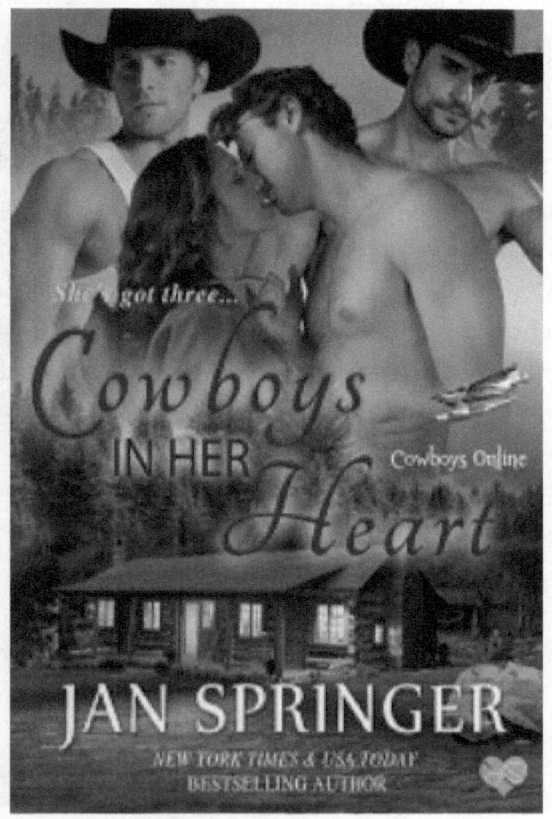

Cowboys In Her Heart
Cowboys Online #4

* * ✿ * *

*AFTER SPENDING TEN years in a maximum-security prison, JJ gets unexpected parole and a job on a Canadian ranch serving up scrumptious dinners and lots of hot love to three of the sexiest cowboys she's ever met.*

Jennifer Jane "JJ" Watson has never been happier. She's going to have a baby!

Thankfully their wilderness ranch is a nice distraction for her three sexy cowboys while she's away flying her plane. But when she's home, her dominant hunks are tending to her naughty pregnant cravings and that includes plenty of sizzling ménages.

Rafe, Brady and Dan don't much like the idea of their woman flying the Canadian skies and being at the mercy of the unpredictable Northern Ontario weather. They would prefer having her warming their beds twenty-four seven. But she has a way of getting what she wants and right now she needs her new-found freedom.

Worst fears are realized when JJ, her friend and JJ's plane suddenly go missing and she doesn't come back home to them.

Always Her Cowboys
Cowboys Online #5

*Rafe, Brady and Dan thought they were getting male ex-cons to help out around their secluded ranch, but instead they get an attractive and very appealing female. In the snowbound wilds of Northern Ontario, female companionship is rare. It's a good thing the three men like to share...*

CHRISTMAS IS COMING once again to Moose Ranch and with the due date of JJ's baby approaching fast, JJ is distracting herself from anxiety attacks by keeping herself ultra-busy preparing for the arrival of her baby and planning Moose Ranch's first annual Christmas party!

In having a wee baby on the way, there's a lot of stress for Brady, Rafe and Dan. Especially due to JJ's decision on having a wilderness mid-wife deliver the baby at the ranch house - *with* all *of them present for the birth*! But their concerns don't stop the men from showing JJ how much they love her...out of bed and in!

With wicked snowstorms, a grounded bush plane, a cheerful holiday party and a sweet little baby, the owners of Moose Ranch know this will be one sparkling Christmas season they won't soon forget...

FUTURISTIC EROTIC ROMANCE (m/f)

Pleasure Bound ~ The Complete Set ~ Books 1-6

A Hero's Welcome – Book One – Dr. Annie welcomes injured astronaut Joe Hero into her bed every chance she gets.

A Hero Escapes – Book Two – Queen Jacey's forbidden fantasies become reality and she can't get enough of well-hung Ben Hero's sizzling lovemaking.

A Hero Betrayed – Book Three – Fugitive-on-the-run Virgin must save Buck Hero who has been infected by a deadly virus. The cure?

A twenty-four-hour making love marathon! But then she must betray him...

A Hero's Kiss – Book Four – US Astronaut Piper Hero is rescued by a dangerous stranger and can't . Why can't seem to keep her hands off his luscious whip-scarred body.

A Hero Wanted – Book Five – A Hero is wanted for plus-sized Jenna who is finally able to explore her intimate side...where menages are welcome.

Captive Heroes – Book Six – While searching for her brothers, Kayla Hero is bound and imprisoned by the Breeders— along with a male captive whose tantalizing scars pique her interest.

Injured and lost in a dense jungle, Kinley Hero is intimidated by the scarred man who hunts her, especially due to the power of erotic submission he holds over her.

Naughty Girl Desires Boxed Set
Contemporary Erotic Romance (m/f)
Includes: Jade's Fantasy, The Biker & The Bride,
Sinderella Sexy and Nice Girl Naughty.

• • ❧ • •

Jade's Fantasy
*In the land of the rich and famous, Kidnap Fantasies is the answer to*
*discreet naughty downtime.*
When ex-downhill skier Jade Hart's two sisters give her a Kidnap
Fantasies questionnaire, Jade is aroused at the prospect of having
no-strings fun in the sun with a stranger whose only job would be to
fulfill her every intimate fantasy. Although she knows she's too shy to
send it in, she secretly pours her deepest wishes into the questionnaire.
Soon the questionnaire mysteriously vanishes and Jade's fantasy man
appears on her luxury yacht in the form of a sexy handy man who gives
her an intimate toy-filled Christmas holiday she'll never forget.

• • ❧ • •

The Biker & The Bride
Wrapped in red-hot lust for revenge, Avery plots to murder the man
responsible for the death of her son.
Her plans are dashed when her ex-husband crashes her wedding and
whisks her away on his motorcycle to the rustic Canadian wilderness
cabin they'd once honeymooned.
Police detective, Mason is fighting for Avery's love with everything he
has.
Armed with whipped cream, handcuffs and his undying devotion,
Mason vows he will make Avery love again.
But it's only a matter of time before the man she'd planned to kill
hunts them down...

· · ✿ · ·

Sinderella Sexy

By night, Dr. Ella Cinder, escapes reality by secretly performing in her own naughty version of Cinderella, aptly re-titled Sinderella. When sexy colleague Dr. Roarke Stephenson appears in the Sinderella audience on the same night her Prince Charming stands her up, Ella Cinder seizes the opportunity to make the man she's secretly fantasized about into her very own Prince Charming for one night of carnal fun in front of an audience.

But at the stroke of midnight, Ella knows she must face the harsh reality that Roarke can never learn her true identity.

Dr. Roarke Stephenson is immediately captured by the mysterious actress who hides her face behind a mask and is known only as Sinderella. For some insane reason, she reminds him of his klutzy co-worker, Ella. But that's not possible. Plain Ella would never have the nerve to do the wickedly delicious things Sinderella does to him, or would she?

· · ✿ · ·

Nice Girl Naughty

Blind since nineteen, Summer has blossomed into a famous wood carver.

When she's almost killed by a serial killer, she's whisked away to a secluded wilderness cabin by the man she once secretly loved.

Summer can't get enough of touching professional bodyguard Nick Cassidy's thick, powerful muscles and all those other hard, yummy male body parts that she has always longed to explore.

For years Nick has stayed away from his best friend's kid sister, nice girl Summer. Now he's back, and sweeping his gorgeous redhead into the naughty cravings he's always had for her. With passion blinding him, Nick doesn't realize their hideout isn't safe—until it's too late.

•• ∼✠∽ ••

YOU CAN GET A PEEK at more of Jan Springer's Erotic Romances at:

http://www.janspringer.com[1]

---

1.     http://www.janspringer.com/

Here are other ways we can connect:

Jan Springer Website at http://www.janspringer.com[2]

Instagram – http://www.instagram.com/janspringerauthor

Facebook - https://www.facebook.com/janspringereroticromance

Twitter - https://twitter.com/janspringer @janspringer

Pinterest - http://www.pinterest.com/janspringer1/

Jan's Blog - http://janspringerauthor.wordpress.com/blog-2/

LinkedIn - http://ca.linkedin.com/in/janspringerauthor/

Google Plus - https://plus.google.com/u/0/101527334949931513035/posts

Goodreads - https://www.goodreads.com/author/show/260628.Jan_Springer

Happy Reading,
Jan Springer

Jan's Newsletter

Hi! If you would like to get an email when my books are released, you can sign up here:

English Newsletter: http://ymlp.com/xguembmugmgb

Your email addresses will never be shared and you can unsubscribe whenever you like.

.. ⚜ ..

Spunky Girl Publishing Erotica
~Jasmine Black~

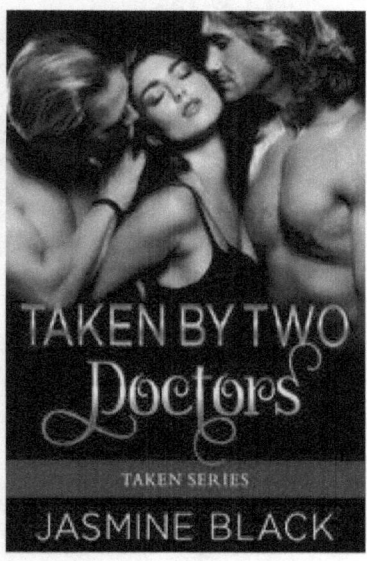

A BDSM Medical Fetish Erotica Quickie MFM
Waitress Jean Spelling, visits her controversial doctor once a month
for some much-needed...stress relief. She looks forward to putting her
feet up in the stirrups and enjoys Dr. Ball's naughty unconventional
treatments. This time when she arrives, she's surprised to discover that
she'll be physically examined by two doctors and they'll prescribe her
some much-needed release right there on the examination table!

• • ❧ • •

Other eBooks in the Taken series
Taken by Two Firefighters
Taken by Two Bikers
Taken by Two Billionaires
Taken by Two Bosses
Taken by Two Cowboys

Taken by Two Personal Trainers
Taken by Two Carpenters
Taken by Three Bikers

•• ❧ ••

Jasmine Black Website ~ http://www.jasmine-black.com
Twitter ~ @blackerotica1

ABOUT THE AUTHOR

Jan Springer writes full-time at her home nestled in cottage country, Ontario, Canada. She enjoys hiking, kayaking, gardening, reading and writing. She is a member of the Romance Writers of America.